THE PRESIDENT'S DAUGHTER

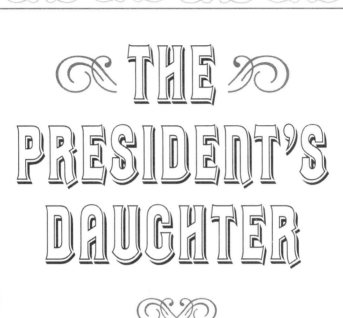

THE PRESIDENT'S DAUGHTER

KIMBERLY BRUBAKER BRADLEY

Delacorte Press

Published by
Delacorte Press
an imprint of
Random House Children's Books
a division of Random House, Inc.
New York

Visit us on the Web! www.randomhouse.com/kids
Educators and librarians, for a variety of teaching tools, visit us at
www.randomhouse.com/teachers

Library of Congress Cataloging-in-Publication Data

Bradley, Kimberly Brubaker.
The President's daughter / Kimberly Brubaker Bradley.
p. cm.
Summary: A fictionalized account of ten-year-old Ethel Roosevelt's early
experiences in the White House after her father, Theodore Roosevelt,
becomes president in 1901.
ISBN 0-385-73147-7 (trade)—ISBN 0-385-90179-8 (GLB)
1. Derby, Ethel Roosevelt—Juvenile fiction. [1. Derby, Ethel Roosevelt—
Fiction. 2. Roosevelt, Theodore, 1858–1919—Fiction. 3. Presidents—
Family—Fiction. 4. United States—History—1901–1909—Fiction.] I. Title.
PZ7.B7247Pr 2004 [Fic]—dc22
2003019018

The text of this book is set in 12-point Goudy.
Book design by Trish Parcell Watts
Printed in the United States of America
November 2004
10 9 8 7 6 5 4 3 2 1
BVG

THE PRESIDENT'S DAUGHTER

Father's foot swung back and forth, tick, tock, tick, tock, in time with the clock on the wall. It was nearly ten o'clock at night. Tuesday, September 13, 1901. We were assembled in the parlor of the main lodge of the Tahawus Club, a resort in the Adirondack Mountains in upper New York State. Usually I would have been asleep already, but not that night. We were waiting for a telegram.

Father stared hard at the page of the book he was reading, almost hard enough to make the words pop off the page. I half expected them to—Father could do anything—but I knew better.

He turned the page. He turned another. Page after page, so fast I knew he wasn't really reading, though Father read faster than anyone I knew, faster even than Mother, who read all the time. Father did everything fast.

He hated waiting. We all did.

Mother looked up from her own book. She said, "Wouldn't you feel better if—"

"Not hardly!" Father snapped. "I'm not going until I'm

sent for. Been there once already. I'd be like an old vulture, hovering over him. Dreadful."

Normally Father wouldn't cut Mother off like that, and she wouldn't stand for it if he did. But that night Father smacked another page of his book and Mother just shook her head. "His poor wife," she murmured. "What on earth will she do?"

I didn't ask whom she meant. I knew. I might have been only ten years old, but I paid attention to everything. Mrs. McKinley, the president's wife, was an invalid. At state dinners the president had to sit beside her, instead of across the table the way he was supposed to, so that if she had an epileptic fit he could cover her face with his napkin. At the inaugural ball, my big sister, Alice, sat on the arm of Mrs. McKinley's chair without ever noticing that Mrs. McKinley was sitting in it. Afterward Sister told Mother that she hadn't meant to be rude.

I didn't get to go to the ball, but I did meet Mrs. McKinley at the inauguration, before the swearing in. She was so lifeless and still, she reminded me of one of Quentin's wax dolls. President McKinley was kind but not joyful. Sister said he had the personality of a mackerel. "Next to him," she said, "Father's brighter than the sun."

Next to most people Father was brighter than the sun. So was Sister, for that matter.

I had wondered if Mrs. McKinley would talk more when she wasn't surrounded by crowds. I had wondered if she would invite Mother to tea in the fall; maybe I could go too. Now I guessed not. A week before, President McKinley had

been shot in the stomach while attending the Pan-
American Exposition in Buffalo, New York. At first everyone had thought he was going to recover, but now it looked
as if they were wrong.

Quentin, my littlest brother, who ought to have been in
bed two hours before, climbed onto Father's knee. "Are you
an old vulture?" he shouted. "Or are you a *bear?*"

Quentin was only three. He didn't understand. Father
played bear with Quentin and Archie, and sometimes with
Kermit and me, almost every night. Not that night,
though. Archie, who was seven, looked up from the parlor
rug with grave anxiety. Archie did understand.

"I'll take him, sir." Mame, our ancient Irish nurse, rose
from the sofa and held out her arms. Quentin ducked and
tried to bury himself beneath Father's elbow. Father
wrapped his arms around Quentin.

"He can stay," Mother said softly. "Just for tonight,
Mame. If you're tired, go ahead to bed. I'll take care of the
children." Mame hesitated, but her back had been hurting
all day. She went out of the parlor. I could hear her steps
down the hall, and the front door opening and shutting.
The cabin we were staying in was just across from the main
lodge.

Quentin fell asleep. Father adjusted his spectacles,
moved Quentin more securely into the crook of his arm,
and shut his book. His crossed foot still swung in the air.
Tick, tock.

Archie reenacted the battle of Kettle Hill with his tin
soldiers on the rug. The rest of us sprawled across the sofas

and chairs. We were taking up the entire parlor, and I hoped none of the other guests minded. We'd come to the Adirondacks for two weeks of vaction after Archie caught chicken pox, Quentin stuck a mothball up his nose, Sister got an abscess in her jaw, Ted got bronchitis, Quentin got an ear infection, I got poison ivy, and Mother almost had a breakdown. Father had been away much of the summer giving speeches, but he'd joined us three days before. The day before, Kermit and I had hiked with him halfway up Mount Marcy and stayed overnight in a hunting cabin. In the morning it was raining, and the first telegram came, saying that President McKinley was worse.

"Why haven't the other guests come into the parlor?" I asked.

"They could if they wished to," Mother said.

"Respect," my oldest brother, Ted, said. "Privacy."

"They weren't worried about privacy before," I said. On the first day Father got there, all the guests and staff lined up to shake his hand. He told them the story of the cougar he killed on his last hunting trip to the Badlands, and they applauded. It was a good story, but I thought they would have applauded a bad one too. Everywhere we went, people wanted to talk to Father.

Kermit, who was almost twelve, put down his book of poetry and looked at me.

"What?" I said.

"Think," he said.

I frowned. "Does everyone here know why we're waiting?"

4

"I imagine so," he said.

I pursed my lips at him. Sometimes Kermit had too much imagination.

"Nonsense," muttered Father.

"Yes," Mother murmured. "Yes, Ethel. They do."

Ted's face twitched. This was his fourteenth birthday, a fact that had gotten lost after the morning's news even though we'd tried to celebrate it at dinner. Ted was Father's namesake, a hard thing to be. None of us could match Father, but I knew Ted felt obliged to try.

Kermit's lips moved softly as he went back to his book. Kermit never could keep poetry to himself. I was halfway through a splendid new book called *Uncle Remus*, but the air in the room didn't feel right to me, and I kept looking up, looking around. I saw Ted twitch again. He wore glasses. The overhead lamp reflected off them and hid the expression in his eyes.

"I wish Sister were here," I said. "She ought to be." Alice was seventeen, the oldest of us all. We always called her Sister. Her real mother, Father's first wife, had been named Alice too, and after she died Father didn't like the name Alice anymore. Mother had never liked it in the first place.

Father looked up and smiled. His white teeth caught the light. "She'd be pacing this room like a caged tiger," he said. I was sure that was right. Just like Father, Sister didn't sit still.

Mother smiled too, but without warmth. "I'm sure she'd rather be having fun," she said.

"I don't think so," I said.

"You can tell her all about it later," whispered Miss Young. "About the waiting, and everything. You can write her a letter." Miss Young gave my arm a squeeze. She was our governess, Sister's and mine, the only thing we shared. Sister really didn't need a governess anymore, though she liked Miss Young almost as much as I did. On her last birthday Sister got her own maid and now she didn't have to study or do anything but have fun. She went away to parties for weeks at a time, always at the homes of the Four Hundred. When I asked Mother what Four Hundred meant, she said, "Four Hundred fools." Father said it was a way of naming a certain group of fashionable rich people. We were not rich or fashionable, but neither were we poor or uncouth.

Sister was different from the rest of us. I knew she was fashionable. She loved beautiful clothes. She was richer than the rest of us too, because of her inheritance from her real mother. I once heard Father tell Mother that we had to be nice to Sister in case we ever needed to borrow her money.

The clock wheezed and struck ten. Mother sighed. Quentin snored. Father continued to beat time with his foot. At ten-fifteen the parlor door creaked open. Mr. LaCasse, one of the mountain guides, stood in the opening with a telegram in his hand. "Sir . . . ," he said in a hoarse, uncertain voice. Father leapt up, still holding Quentin, and snatched the telegram. He tore it open. Quentin sighed and nestled himself around Father's neck.

"That's it," Father said. "I must go now." He handed

Quentin to Mother, adjusted his glasses, buttoned his coat. He asked Mr. LaCasse, "You've got horses ready?"

"Three pairs, sir, in stages all the way down, and the light buckboard. But it's raining something fierce now, and the night's black as can be. We've got lanterns on the buckboard. Still, it's a dangerous road."

"Speed," said Father. "That's the only important thing. The faster the better."

It had taken us an entire day to get to the Tahawus Club from the train station in North Creek, the closest village. The road was steep and flinty. In some places it ran along a cliff. I couldn't imagine Father going down it at night.

I would not imagine it. Then I wouldn't worry as much.

Mother lifted her face and Father kissed her. Ted shook his hand. So did Kermit. I hugged him. "Good-bye, dearest Ethel," he said, kissing my ear. "I'll see you in a few days, I'm sure. And I'll write you a letter."

Father wrote me letters whenever he was away. "Be careful," I whispered.

Father lifted Archie and hugged him. Archie burst into tears. "Don't let them shoot you!" he cried. "Don't let them shoot you, too!"

Father put Archie down and knelt on the rug beside him. "Why, Archiekins," he said, "I'm surprised at you." He reached into his pants pocket and showed Archie the pearl handle of his revolver. "Do you really think some old anarchist would be faster on the draw than a cowboy like me?"

I wasn't sure what an anarchist was, except that one had shot President McKinley. I knew, though, that Father was a

7

good cowboy, and proud of it. He had had cattle ranches in the Badlands, before I was born. He even wrote books about the West. Ted said they were best sellers.

Archie shuffled his feet and sniffed. Father waited. "No, Father," Archie said at last.

"If anyone comes at me, I'll get to them first. Don't worry. I'll be fine."

While Father drove off into the dark wet night, Mother packed us all off to bed. I heard her giving orders to Pinckney, Father's valet, and to Annie, her maid. We had planned to stay another week, but now we were to leave at first light.

I rolled over in my bunk and pulled the wool blanket over my head. I shut my eyes tight to keep from crying. I was no better than Archie, I thought. I worried that someone would shoot Father too.

* * *

As soon as we'd finished breakfast the next morning, Mother crammed us all into the lodge's horse cart and we started down the road to the train station. The rain had stopped but the skies were overcast and gloomy. The road was slick in some spots and bumpy in others, and the crowded cart was uncomfortable. Mame moaned. Quentin whined. Ted looked as if he wanted to punch somebody. Mother and Miss Young were tight-lipped. My stomach quivered and flopped.

"Father must have made it down all right," I said. "We'd have heard, wouldn't we, if he'd had an accident?"

Ted sat squashed so close to me that his elbow banged my ribs. "Of course," he said. "Don't be such a fusspot."

"I am not a fusspot," I said. "You know yourself—"

Miss Young shushed me. "Have mercy on your mother, Ethel. Don't get something started."

"But he—" I saw the look on Miss Young's face and stopped. Miss Young never threatened, but, like Mother, she knew how to be firm.

The cart bumped and jolted. "My ear hurts," said Quentin. Nobody shushed him. He pulled at his ear and complained again. Mother turned him in her arms so she could look into his ear. "My goodness, of course it hurts," she said. "You've stuck a pebble into it. Didn't you learn anything from that mothball up your nose?"

"No," whimpered Quentin.

"We'll get you to a doctor when we get home," Mother said. "Shhh, you rest now. Just rest."

Kermit tried to read but the cart jostled his book too much. He slapped the book shut and put it away, glaring at Ted and me as if we were to blame.

"Be grateful," Ted told him. "At least *you* don't have to rush off to Groton." Groton was a boarding school run by one of Father's friends. Ted started there the past year. He hated it, but Father still wanted him to go there. Ted had been supposed to leave for school straight from the Tahawus Club; his trunk had been sent ahead.

"I'll be at Mr. Preston's," said Kermit. "Same difference."

Mr. Preston's was the school in Washington that was going to prepare Kermit for Groton. Archie was young enough to go to a regular public school. Quentin was too young for school, and Alice and I didn't go to school at all; girls didn't have to. That was why we had Miss Young.

"It's not the same," Ted said earnestly. "Groton's dreadful. You wait and see. This will make it worse than ever."

Kermit frowned. Ted frowned. Quentin started to cry again. Only Archie looked at all happy, even though he had been the only one to cry the night before. I wondered whether it was because he trusted Father more than the rest of us, or whether he was just too young to understand how many things could go wrong.

"Do you trust Father?" I asked Kermit.

He looked at me as though I'd asked him if he breathed air. "Of *course*," he said. "We can always trust Father. It's all the other people we have to watch out for."

Father had been shot at before, especially during the Spanish-American War three years earlier. As a colonel in the army, he had led a group of cowboy soldiers called the Rough Riders up San Juan Hill. It was a famous battle, and he had won. He'd ridden his horse straight through enemy fire and had not been harmed. With his letters home he had sent us spent shells from bullets that had missed him.

But in a war, you expected to be shot at. You knew to be careful. All President McKinley had been doing was shaking hands.

"I wish Sister were here," I said again. She wouldn't mope, and if she was worried, we wouldn't be able to tell. Sister would have something interesting to say. She would take our minds off of everything.

"Me too," Miss Young replied.

Mother handed out sandwiches and, when Mame wouldn't eat, made her take sips of water. She promised Mame hot tea the moment we got to the train station. She got Quentin calmed down and asked Kermit to teach Archie to recite a poem by heart. Mother always knew the right things to do. I watched her for a while, and then I asked Ted about the trees we were passing, and the birds and wildflowers, until he started to seem less gloomy. He knew all about birds. When I said so, he shook his head. "Not as much as Father does," he said.

"You know more than most people," I said. "Besides, nobody knows as much about birds as Father."

Father could hear a bird singing in the woods and say exactly what kind it was. When we were out walking, he'd sometimes pick up a single feather from the ground and tell us all about the bird it had come from.

"I know," Ted said, looking gloomy again. "I miss Sister too," he added.

I looked at him sideways. "You do?" He and Sister often did things together, because they were the oldest, but they fought a lot too. They'd had a big fight at the Tahawus Club right before Sister left, and Ted had been awful. I was still a little mad at him.

"Sure. The rest of you all are babies. You don't have any idea what's going to happen to us." He paused. "This changes everything. Our whole lives."

I thought he was wrong about that. At least I hoped so. I liked my life the way it was; I didn't want it to be different. "I'm not a baby," I said. "What do you think will happen?"

11

"Who was vice president before Father?" Ted asked. "Can you remember?"

I thought a moment. "No. I didn't pay any attention," I said.

"It was Garrett Hobart," Ted said. "Remember him?" I shook my head. "He died. But that's what I mean," Ted said. "No one pays attention to the vice president. You'll see. Everything will be different now." He sighed. "Groton will be worse than ever."

"You said that before."

"Well, it's true."

"Are you scared?" I asked.

Ted bristled. "*No.*"

"I don't mean about school," I said. "I mean about Father—"

Just then the wagon rounded the last bend. We'd reached North Creek at last. We pulled up to the station, where a train was waiting at the siding. As soon as the wagon stopped, a man came out of the station and handed a note to Mother. I put my head under her arm but I couldn't read it. The boys jostled close.

"Well," said Mother. I could tell it was something she'd been expecting. "Onto the train now. Let's go." She handed the note to Ted, who read it and passed it to Kermit, who read it and handed it to me.

"What does it say?" Archie asked.

I cleared my throat. "It's from Father," I said. "It says, 'President McKinley died two-fifteen this morning. Theodore Roosevelt.' "

Archie's eyes widened. "Oh," he said. He went to help Ted and Kermit load the bags onto the train. I folded the note and gave it back to Mother, who put it into the pocket of her traveling suit.

It was odd that Father wrote his last name on a note meant for Mother. Sister would say it was a posterity letter, written not just for us but to be saved for history, and maybe she would be right. Father was Theodore Roosevelt. Colonel Roosevelt, the hero of San Juan Hill. Governor Roosevelt, of the state of New York. Since the past March, Vice President Roosevelt, and now, because of an assassin's bullet, President Roosevelt.

President of the United States.

As I climbed onto the train I thought, *Now I am the president's daughter.*

It was a long ride back to Sagamore, our home on Long Island. We had been planning to move to Washington, D.C., in a few weeks, but Mother said that would have to be speeded up now. Still, we had a few days to catch our breath at Sagamore, and I was glad. No matter where else we lived, we always came home to Sagamore. I loved the fields and the orchard there; I loved swimming in the sound. I loved Cooper's Bluff, the sand cliff Father always led us down on our scrambles. I loved the huge barn where Father built us obstacle courses through the hay, and I loved Christmas mornings in the big drafty parlor. I loved the way the air smelled at Sagamore. I'd heard Mother say that the air in Washington was choky and thick.

Everything was different now. Instead of the little house we'd planned to rent for Father's vice presidency, we would be living in the Executive Mansion.

"Just think," I said, "it's the same house George Washington lived in." I tried to feel excited, but I didn't, not yet.

"Is not," said Kermit.

"Is too!" I kicked him.

"Is not," Ted cut in. "Washington never lived in it, Ethie. Adams did."

"Oh."

"Adams was the second president. John Adams."

"I know *that*," I said. "Well, we'll be staying in the same house Lincoln did."

"Yes, we will," Miss Young said encouragingly.

"You are still coming, aren't you?" I asked. Pinckney, Annie, and Mame always came wherever we went, and usually our cook came too. The housemaids and grooms sometimes came and sometimes didn't; the gardeners never did. I didn't know about Miss Young. She'd only been with us since Albany.

"I think so. Your mother and I will discuss it," said Miss Young.

Quentin had laid his head in Mame's lap. Both of them looked terrible. Quentin's face was red, and he kept digging at the ear with the pebble in it. Mame looked white and groaned whenever the train rattled especially hard. "Mame's still coming," Quentin murmured.

"Oh, Quenty, I don't know," Mame said. "I'm such an old woman now."

"You're not old," he said. "You're comfy."

She patted him, but I was alarmed. Mame had been coming to the rented house for sure. I knew she was old— she had been Mother's nurse—but we needed her. If she didn't come to the Executive Mansion, who on earth would take care of Archie and Quentin? And if Miss Young wasn't there, who would take care of me?

Mame shuddered, and Quentin cried out again. Mother

took him onto her lap. I'd ask Mother about it later, I decided.

Archie's hat had slid down over one eye. He was sitting next to a window and looking out with a dreamy expression. I didn't think he was seeing anything at all. "Algonquin," he said, and smiled.

Algonquin was our calico pony. We had all learned to ride on him, but Archie loved him best.

I didn't pay Archie any mind. Kermit was reading a newspaper he'd gotten at North Creek, and I held out my hand for it.

"The president," Archie continued, more loudly now, "must be a very important man."

"Yes," said Ted, "but so must the vice president. Anyhow, it's still just Father. Don't get a big head."

Archie shot Ted a look but otherwise ignored him. "The president," he continued, "must be a very important man, with very, very large stables. The president would have room for Algonquin in his very large stables in Washington, D.C."

"Ah," said Kermit. When Father was vice president we couldn't afford to bring Algonquin to Washington. Mother said livery board in the capital was expensive; all our horses except Father's and Mother's saddle horses and one carriage pair were going to have to stay at Sagamore.

"I bet that's right," I said. "I bet the mansion has a big stable." Archie and I grinned at each other. I loved horses too. If the president had his own stable, I thought, then we could take Algonquin, Yagenka, Renown, Texas, Diamond, and Wyoming, the horse I usually rode. Maybe even both carriage pairs. "Mother?" I asked. "Will we need both carriage pairs?"

Mother looked up. She had been writing notes to herself. "At least," she said. "And yes, Archie, Algonquin may come."

"He'll love Washington," Archie said, "and I will ride him to school every day."

"What about Wyoming?" I asked.

"Yes," Mother said. "Yes, I'm sure we can bring Wyoming."

The news didn't make Ted or Kermit all that happy. They knew they'd be spending most of their time at school. But Archie and I grinned and grinned. Washington, D.C., seemed much more interesting now that I knew I could ride there.

* * *

Every time we stopped at a station, Ted or Kermit ran out and bought an extra newspaper so that we could read more and more about Father as we went. He had taken the oath of office in Buffalo, New York, where President McKinley's Cabinet had assembled once his death seemed certain. Father's inaugural speech to the Cabinet was the shortest one ever. The paper reprinted it. Kermit read it aloud.

"It shall be my aim to continue absolutely unbroken the policies—"

"Is it a good speech?" Ted asked Mother anxiously. He sat very upright on the train's velvet seat. It was nighttime now. We would sleep on the train and reach New York City midmorning.

"What do you think?" Mother asked.

"Yes," said Kermit. "He said what he meant and sat down." Father believed in quick words, punchy language.

Quentin slept with his head in Mame's lap. Mame looked more and more unwell. "Madam," she said, "will you need me immediately in Washington?" Her voice quavered.

"Oh, my," Mother said. She looked at Mame sympathetically. "Not at first, I'm sure. I'll have to send for you, Mame, once I find out how things are."

"If you're sure, madam," Mame said. I could tell she was relieved.

"No Mame?" said Quentin.

I saw Mother glance at Miss Young, and saw Miss Young nod the smallest bit. She put her arm around Quentin. "It'll be all right," she told him. "It will."

I hoped so. Too many things were changing.

Monday morning, the day before President McKinley's funeral, I woke very early and watched as Mother, all dressed in black, sipped a cup of tea and waited for the carriage to be brought around. She was taking the first train to Washington. "Will you see Father?" I asked her. Outside, clouds blanketed the still-dark sky. I sat beside Mother on the bench in the front hall and wrapped the hem of my nightgown around my cold toes.

"Yes, of course," she said. She pushed my hair back from my forehead and kissed me. "I'll tell him you send your love. Take care of things while I'm gone, will you? Take care of Mame."

"Yes, ma'am." The doctor had come the day before. He'd removed the pebble from Quentin's ear and told Mame that she had a kidney infection, a bad one. It was no wonder her back had hurt so much. Mame wouldn't be able to go to Washington anytime soon. "I'll take care of everything," I promised. Ted had left for school already, so I was second oldest after Kermit. Mother could count on me.

"Thank you." Mother brushed her lips against my forehead again, and then the carriage pulled up and she left, her head bent against the strong wind as she walked out the door.

I got dressed and checked to see that everything was all right in the kitchens. Our cook was making breakfast. I poured a fresh cup of tea and took it up to Mame.

"Thank you, dear." Mame lay propped by pillows. She looked very tired, and the wrinkles on her forehead were deep. "Your mother's gone?"

"Yes, ma'am."

"I thought I heard the horses."

"I wish I could have gone with her," I said.

"To the funeral?" Mame said. "Dear heart, you don't want to see that. It'll be a sad, sad time."

That was why I wanted to see Father so badly. I wanted to know how he was now that he was president. Father had not changed much when he went from being governor to vice president, though he had been a little less happy. Would he be happy now? Could he be happy, when everyone was so sad? The newspaper was full of stories, how President McKinley's friends had wept at his bedside and begged him not to die. Some of the Cabinet members had wanted to quit, but Father had convinced them all to stay.

"Is it bad luck, Father becoming president this way?" Mame knew all about luck. Her bedtime stories were full of fairies and magic.

Mame shook her head. "A body makes its own luck, Ethel. Your father must have been destined to be president.

Why else would he have been vice president?" She sighed and handed me back the teacup. "Go on now, darling. Let this old woman rest."

I ate breakfast, then went outside. Kermit was partway up the windmill, straddling one of the crosspieces. Our windmill was tall but easy to climb. The boards were thick and you could grab them. I stuck my toes against the lowest board and pulled myself up. My dress caught on a splinter and tore a little. I pulled it loose and scooted next to Kermit.

"Hello," he said quietly. "I'm watching Archie and Quentin." I looked down. They were wrestling on the dew-wet lawn. They were both naked except for their short pants, and pieces of wet grass stuck to them.

"They're playing assassination," Kermit said. "First Archie is the assassin, and Quentin tackles him and saves Father. Then Quentin is the assassin, and Archie tackles him and saves Father."

I nodded. "What would you do?"

Kermit turned his pale eyes toward me. "If there was an assassin? I'd tackle him and save Father."

"Me too," I said. I moved closer to Kermit. "Do you re-member what that one man said in the paper? When every-one else was trying to make Father be the vice president?"

Kermit grinned. "Which man? Which paper? There are such an awful lot of them, and they say such awful things." Father said we were never, not ever, to believe what we saw printed in any newspaper without checking with him first.

"About why Father shouldn't have been vice president."

Kermit's face clouded. "You mean, 'Don't any of you realize there's only one life between this madman and the presidency?' Senator Hanna said that."

"I was thinking about it," I said. "Because it turned out to be true."

"One life," Kermit said. "Yes. But Father's not a madman. He'll be a good president."

"Why doesn't Senator Hanna like him?"

"I don't know." Kermit shifted his seat. "Politics, I guess. He liked McKinley. He thinks Father's a cowboy."

"Father *is* a cowboy." I knew all about his adventures on his cattle ranches. He used to brand calves during the spring roundup, and he shot panthers and tracked down thieves. It was true he'd lost most of his money when the cattle died in a blizzard before I was born, but Mother always said that what Father gained was more important than money. She said Father had been sick all the time when he was a boy, and that he was not strong when he was first grown up. Working on the ranch gave him his health, something money couldn't buy. Being a cowboy had saved him. I thought it was something people liked about him. A lot of the Rough Riders had come from out West and joined up just because of Father. "So why is that a bad thing?" I asked Kermit.

He squirmed. "They don't mean cowboy the way you mean cowboy," he said. "They mean somebody who's rough, who doesn't take baths or use good manners."

"Oh, but that's not Father."

"I know," Kermit said. "But I think some people feel— well, there's businesses, you know, that make a lot of money, because they've got things set up so no one else can compete with them. They're monopolies, like the railroads, or the steel companies. Father thinks they ought to be regulated. The people who run the businesses don't like that."

On the lawn below us, Archie and Quentin were punching each other. I couldn't tell who was supposed to be the assassin. "What's 'regulated'?" I asked.

"Controlled," said Kermit. "With laws. Something like that. You'll have to ask Ted. Or ask Father, he won't mind. It's complicated."

I sighed. "Do you think Father'll like being president?"

"Better than he liked being vice president, I'm sure."

Father had not wanted to be vice president. Mother had not wanted it for him. Sister, who had gone with them to the nominating convention, had been disgusted by the very idea. Father would have refused if he had known how, because he thought he was being asked to be vice president to keep him from continuing as governor of New York. When Father was governor he got to make a lot of decisions about important things. As vice president, he didn't get to.

"Where's Senator Hanna now?"

"In the Senate, silly. He's from Ohio." Kermit swung down off his plank. He reached for me and helped me jump down. "Let's go feed the guinea pigs. I'm taking them all to Washington."

* * *

Archie cried out in his sleep at night. Quentin insisted on having all the dogs in bed with him, under the covers, even

23

though the nights were still warm. We made black arm-bands for our dolls to wear, out of respect for President McKinley. Archie made one for Algonquin, but Algonquin didn't like it and kept stamping it off. Finally Kermit made Archie stop trying to put it back on. He said it was ridiculous to put animals into mourning. I kept an eye on the household, as Mother had asked, and tried not to miss her and Father.

* * *

On Wednesday morning we read the newspaper accounts of President McKinley's funeral as we waited for Mother to come home. Father had ridden with President McKinley's body on a special funeral train all the way from Buffalo to Washington. At every station along the way, men and women stood in lines along the tracks. Bands played hymns in honor of the dead president, and women laid flowers on the rails. When the train pulled in, Father would stand on the platform at the back of the train, a black armband over his sleeve and his hat in his hand, and silently acknowledge the crowd. Once, as they entered Washington, people began to cheer him. Father's head snapped up, and he glared so fiercely that the noise stopped instantly. No one should cheer a funeral train. Father knew better.

It rained throughout the funeral service. Poor Mrs. McKinley could hardly stand. After eating dinner with Mother, Father got back onto the train with President McKinley's body to escort it to Canton, Ohio, for burial.

It was raining at Sagamore, too, and gray and cold. The

postman had brought the mail along with the newspaper, and Miss Young sorted it at the breakfast table, setting aside some letters but opening many others herself. "My goodness," she said, shaking her head, "your mother will need a secretary. Listen. The editors of *Ladies' Home Journal* wish to photograph all of you children for an article on America's new First Family, to be published as soon as possible. The editors of the *Washington Post* wish to know where the young Roosevelt children will attend school. The headmaster of Groton writes that he has received several requests to interview Ted and will deny them all until he receives instructions to the contrary." She shook her head. "Poor Ted."

Mame was still in bed, so Miss Young was presiding at the table. Kermit sat at the foot, in Father's place. He whistled. Miss Young smiled. "Then there are the letters from schools. Fully nine private academies in Washington have offered their services, countless tutors—"

I spoke up. "I don't need a school. Sister and I have you."

Miss Young smiled. "I've enjoyed our studies, dear. But a school might be a nice environment for Alice and you. The Executive Mansion may be a lonely place."

Archie laughed. "Not with us in it," he said.

* * *

When Mother came home she had answers for everything. A president needed a lot of carriage horses, so Father was going to buy three more pairs to keep in Washington, and we were going to leave both of our current pairs at

Sagamore to use whenever we were home. All the other horses would come with us to Washington. "Except Pony Grant," Mother said. "Pony Grant is too old." We had had him forever; Sister's other grandparents had bought him for her before I was born.

We could take all the guinea pigs, as well as Eli Yale, Sister's macaw, and Emily Spinach, Sister's snake. We could take Tom Quartz, our new kitten, and Kermit's kangaroo rat and my rabbits. We could take some of our dogs, but not the ones that would be miserable living in a city. They would stay at Sagamore and live with the carriage horses.

"Has there been a letter from Sister?" Mother asked. I shook my head. Mother pursed her lips and looked disappointed. "Well," she said, "I'm sure we'll hear from her soon. She must be exposed to news in some form, even among the people with whom she currently associates."

Mother began to sort the mail into stacks, putting all the letters from schools to one side. "You know Mame can't come with us," she said to me. I nodded. "Miss Young has graciously agreed to take her place with Archie and Quentin, and . . ." Mother set the mail aside and turned toward me. "Your father and I have decided to send you and Sister to the National Cathedral School for Girls in Washington. It'll be an excellent opportunity for you. You'll get a fine education, and best of all, you'll be able to be home with us every weekend."

My breathing stopped. "What do you mean 'every weekend'?" I said. "School doesn't last all night."

"It's a boarding school," Mother said quietly. "Right inside Washington. Like Mr. Preston's, Kermit's school."

"A boarding school?" I said. I'd never imagined that. "I have to go to a *boarding* school?"

"You'll like it," Mother said. "I truly believe you will. It's been open for only a year, but it has an excellent reputation. And Sister will be there."

Knowing Sister, I doubted it.

I went down to the bay to cry.

Kermit tagged along after me. "Go away," I told him. I sat on the sand and let my bare feet scrunch into it. Tears rolled down my cheeks, and I wiped them on my sleeve. I never cried loudly, but I was often messy about it.

"It won't be so bad," he said.

"It'll be awful. I don't want to go to boarding school! I want to stay home! I want to stay with Miss Young."

Kermit skipped a rock into the water. "It's not any different from what I'm doing."

"Except that you already knew about it," I said. "You were going to go there anyhow. If Father weren't president, I bet they'd let me stay home." I raised my head. "Mother says Sister's going with me."

Kermit cocked his eyebrow. "You believe that?"

Sister had been to school for a total of three months in her entire life. It had been a public day school, not a private or a boarding school. "It was wonderful," she said once, her eyes lighting up. "A whole gang of boys, and

28

me at the head! We had such fun together." Mother's mouth tightened as Sister said it. It was easy to guess why Sister hadn't stayed in that school.

"No," I said. "But I wish she were."

* * *

At first I suffered in silence and only cried at the beach, but no one noticed me, so I got noisier. When Miss Young bought me a trunk to take to school, I started crying at mealtimes. I sulked as much as possible, but Mother still said I had to go. She took me into town and bought me new shoes. I hated them. Miss Young tried to reason with me. I pouted. "Why is no one listening?" I asked. "I don't want to go. I want to stay home."

"We are listening," Miss Young said. "You've made your feelings sufficiently obvious. But you don't have a choice here, dear."

I scowled and kicked the dirt with the new shoes.

"I never knew you to be afraid of anything," Miss Young said.

"I'm not afraid," I said. I just wanted to stay where Father was. I wanted Mother to read to me every night.

"Your parents have decided what's best for you," Miss Young said.

"Would I have to do this if Father weren't the president?"

Miss Young looked sober. "Probably not," she said. "Your family is going to be living a different sort of life now, Ethel. In a little rented house you and I and Archie and

Quentin could do very well together. Not in the Executive Mansion."

I understood, at least a little, even though I didn't want to. Every day we got more and more letters from newspapers and magazines asking about me and Sister and the boys. They'd never done that before. But understanding didn't mean I was any happier about it. I liked the life we had.

The day before Mother took Kermit and me to Washington, I got a letter from Sister. I was playing on the beach by the sound when Miss Young brought it to me.

I recognized Sister's handwriting on the envelope at once. I smiled. "Did Mother get one too?"

Miss Young shook her head. "I don't think so. I sorted today's mail."

I sat down on the warm sand to read it. Miss Young sat beside me. When I finished I folded the letter carefully and slid it back into the envelope.

"What's wrong?" Miss Young asked.

I brushed a tear from my cheek. "She's not going to school with me," I said. "She's at Aunt Bamie's and Uncle Will's house in Connecticut, and she says she's staying there. She says don't I remember what happened when they tried to make her go to Miss Spence's School."

"What happened?"

I put the letter in my pocket. I would read it again later, when I was by myself. "It was when Father was first elected governor. Sister told Father she'd disgrace him if he sent her away. She said she'd do something awful." I remembered how Sister's eyes had glittered, how fierce she'd looked, like a cornered wildcat. "I guess they believed her," I went on. "That was when we got you." I sniffed, trying not to cry. I'd never really believed Sister would go to school with me, but I had wanted it so.

Part of me wished I were like her. I could cry about school and I could pout, but I could never do anything shameful. I just couldn't. Father would be so grieved.

Miss Young squeezed my hand. "School's not such an awful thing, Ethel. I went away to school myself. I liked it, after a while."

"After how long?" I asked.

"Not too long," she said. "I know it's hard to go away."

"Sister doesn't want to be with us that much anymore," I said, sliding my hand into the pocket with her letter.

"Aunt Bamie will take good care of her," Miss Young said.

"Sometimes I think Sister feels like she's not part of our family," I said. I scooted closer to Miss Young. The sand was warm and soft. "She had a different mother, you know. One who died."

Miss Young nodded. "I know," she said.

"Aunt Bamie took care of her when she was a baby," I said. "Aunt Bamie loves her."

"Yes, and your mother loves her too," Miss Young said. She stroked my hair back from my forehead. "Sister's not an easy person to be around sometimes."

She was easy for me to be around. She was always easy for me. I stabbed at the sand with my finger. "Before we went to Tahawus, Mother said Sister's real mother was a silly girl who would have bored Father to death if she'd lived."

Miss Young's hand froze against my hair. "She said that to you?" she said. "To Sister?"

"To Ted," I said, gulping back tears. "And Ted told Sister. I heard him." Was it any wonder, I thought, that Sister hadn't come home? "Why would Mother say something like that?"

"She didn't say it to Sister," Miss Young said. "I'm sure she never meant her to hear it. Remember that."

But she had said it to Ted. Mother hadn't cared that Ted had heard it. I loved Mother so, but I loved Sister, too.

Sometimes I felt like the only person in our family who worried about Sister at all.

Miss Young smelled like lilac powder. I leaned against her.

"Sister's mother died two days after Sister was born," I said. "It was the exact same day that Father's mother died in the exact same house."

"I know," Miss Young said. She smoothed my hair from my forehead.

"Father's mother died of typhoid, but I don't think Sister's mother died of that. I don't know why she died." I shrugged. "We aren't allowed to talk about her, you know. Not ever. Aunt Bamie tells Sister about her sometimes, but that's all." I was eight years old before I thought to ask who the woman in Sister's photograph was, and why Mame reminded Sister every night to pray for her dear mother in heaven.

"Some things are best forgotten," Miss Young said.

"I don't think so," I said. We sat silently.

"It's suppertime," Miss Young said when we had watched the waves for a few minutes more, "and then we need to finish packing your things." I helped her up and we started the long slow walk back to the house.

"I shouldn't have told Sister about the school," I said.

"Your mother told her too," Miss Young said. "It isn't your fault."

After supper I went into Sister's room. It was kept very orderly now that she had a maid of her own. The photograph of Sister's mother hung on the wall beside her bed. I took it down from its nail and carried it to Miss Young. "Will you pack this safely?" I asked. "Sister will want it in her room in Washington."

Miss Young took it from me. "Certainly," she said. "What treasures do you want?"

I had dolls and books and games. "It doesn't matter," I said. The things I most wanted I couldn't take with me. Father, Mother, Sister, my brothers, Miss Young. They would be in Washington, but not at my school.

When Mrs. McKinley moved out of the Executive Mansion a few days after the funeral, Mother and Kermit and I moved in. We left Archie and Quentin behind at Sagamore with Miss Young until we had a chance to get settled. I loved traveling so cozily, with Mother, Kermit, the two maids, the cook, and me all snug in one corner of the swinging train car. The trip to Washington, D.C., passed quickly. My two white rabbits were quite patient in their basket, and Kermit's kangaroo rat didn't seem to mind in the least being on a train. He hopped in and out of Kermit's pocket while Mother read bits from *Pride and Prejudice* that Kermit said were funny. I didn't think so.

"You have to be older to understand," Kermit said.

"Do not," I said.

"Do so," he said. "You'd better hope so, anyhow. Otherwise it's not that you're too young, it's that you're too thick in the head."

I stuck my tongue out at Kermit. I could've kicked him. Then I started to worry. What if I *was* thick in the head?

Probably all the girls at school had read *Pride and Prejudice* and thought it was so amusing they laughed themselves silly. I scowled.

"That's enough," said Mother. She marked her place and set the book aside.

The rhythm of the wheels changed as the train began to slow for Union Station. "Listen," I said, "doesn't the train sound like *Father, Father, Father*—"

"Yes," said Mother, listening. "Yes, I suppose it does." She had put on a somber dress, because of President McKinley, but it was one of Father's favorites. She looked beautiful and trim. I knew just how Father would smile when he saw her. I knew just how happy he'd be.

* * *

When the train stopped, Mother arranged for our trunks and crates and the horses to be unloaded and sent to the president's house. Kermit buttoned his rat into his coat pocket and bundled his books together. I took my rabbits in their basket. Annie gathered up the rest of our things. Then Mother hired a cab and we all climbed aboard. Evening had come and the light was fading from the indigo sky. The Capitol gleamed white above the rooftops of the buildings around it. The horses clip-clopped slowly through the almost-empty streets. There were no crowds, no cheering, no one to notice us at all. I breathed deep. The air carried the scent of autumn: warm dry leaves, damp earth.

Sooner than I expected, the carriage pulled up to the Executive Mansion. It was a huge building, square and white, much grander than I had expected, but I hardly noticed it at all. Up the steps, in the gaslit doorway, stood Father.

Kermit and I fell over each other as we rushed out of the carriage. Kermit was first onto the ground but I jumped over him, and we scrambled to our feet and ran—*wham!*—straight into Father, wonderful Father. He met us partway down the stairs, caught us both around our middles, and lifted us off the ground.

"Father!" I said. He smelled so perfectly the same.

"Sweet Ethel," he said, kissing the top of my head. "Dear Kermit. My, how I've missed you! And here's Mother! As lovely as ever." He set me down, drew Mother toward him, and kissed her full on the lips. "Come on!" he said, herding us toward the open door. "You'll want to see the place. It needs work, Edie—" The fading sunlight glinted off his glasses and his teeth as he smiled. "Oh, this house is a disaster."

"Well," Mother said cheerfully, "it won't be for long."

The president's house made the governor's mansion in Albany, with its fusty furniture and terrible old wallpaper, look like a palace fit for a king. "It hasn't been fixed up in ever so long," Father explained as he walked us through the door. Mother sniffed. I did too. It smelled musty, like our cellar at Sagamore. "Congress put some money aside to re-decorate," Father continued, "but McKinley never got the chance to spend it. I'm sure we'll set the place to rights."

Mother stopped in her tracks. "That," she said, "will be the first thing to go."

The rest of us stopped too. "That" was a wall directly in front of us made up entirely of pieces of colored glass. It filled the space between the columns of the entrance hall, top to bottom, side to side, all the way down the hallway. Bright reds, blues, and greens blazed in the fading sunlight. Looking closely, I could see American flags and eagles intertwined in some of the panes. It was shockingly ugly, almost hideous. I giggled.

Father cleared his throat. "It was made by Tiffany. President Arthur put it in, to stop drafts. I believe they say it's in the Arabian style." He looked at Mother. "Don't know that you'd have it be the *first* thing out, though. After all, you haven't seen upstairs."

Kermit said, "Look at the hen!"

On a table in the vestibule a china hen sat on a nest of china eggs. I ran up to touch her.

"Another relic," Father said, waving cheerily to an old man who stood near the door. "Been here forever, so they say." I thought Father meant that the man was a relic, but then I realized he was talking about the hen.

"Out," Mother said, laughing a little. "China hen, second thing to go."

The old man smiled and waved at Kermit and me. I waved back. "Hello, Mr. Pendel," Father said. The man was wearing a uniform, so I guessed he was a doorman or some other kind of servant.

Father was already striding away. I ran to catch up. "Are there guards here?" I asked him.

He frowned. "Heavens, yes. Uniformed policemen following me everywhere. A lot of time-wasting nonsense."

Kermit and Mother and I grinned at each other. We

hoped for lots of policemen. Attentive policemen. Better policemen than President McKinley had had.

Beyond the glass wall was another wide hallway, full of old sofas and tattered chairs. It looked like the parlor of a train station. Then Father led us into an immense open room. Giant ancient chandeliers hung from a painted red and gold ceiling. The carpet was so threadbare we could have skated on it. Enormous O-shaped sofas, with potted palms stuck in their middles, stood at intervals beneath the chandeliers. "The East Room," Father said.

"Wow," said Kermit with a shudder.

"How awful," said Mother.

I didn't say anything. I'd never expected the Executive Mansion to be so gloomy. I'd hoped it would be homey, like Sagamore. But Mother strode the length of the room and swept the heavy curtains aside. She began to throw the windows open. It was twilight, but the room seemed suddenly lighter. A breeze ruffled the leaves on the potted palms.

Father smiled. "I knew you'd put it to rights," he said.

Mother said, "This is just a beginning."

Father led us through the Green Room, the Blue Room, the Red Room. "Is there a Purple Room?" I asked hopefully. "Lavender? Yellow?"

"Yellow makes the ladies look bilious," Father said, laughing.

Mother shook her head. "So does that particular shade of green."

We went through the State Dining Room—Mother opened more windows—and then up a little stairway with a carved-eagle balustrade, the first thing in the whole mansion that reminded me of Sagamore. I ran my hand over the eagle fondly. "This is private," Father said. "The public stairs are at the opposite end."

"Public stairs to the family quarters?" Mother raised her eyebrows. The public didn't go upstairs at the governor's mansion in Albany.

Father coughed but didn't say anything.

The upstairs hallway was wide and long and the ceiling was wonderfully high, but the carpet was horrible and the wallpaper was worse. Sofas and tables lined the walls. "These are our rooms," Father was saying. Mother opened one door, peeked in, then opened another.

"My," she said, "it's like living over the store." She pointed down the hallway. "What's beyond those glass doors?"

Father coughed again. "Offices. My office, in fact. Everyone's offices."

"Well," Mother said. She opened and shut a few more doors. "Is this all the room we have?" Father nodded. "I'm sure it can be changed," Mother said. "Though where we'll put everyone to start is more than I know." She smiled at me. "What do you think, Ethel? Do you suppose it's a good thing Ted's at Groton?"

I had been eager to look through all the rooms, hoping to be allowed to chose my own. Mother's words caught me short. "No," I said, scowling. "No, I don't." I knew she meant to be funny, but it didn't strike me as amusing at all. Pretty soon I'd be gone too. Whatever room I got would be empty most of the time.

Mother picked out her and Father's bedroom first, a big one right at the top of the stairs. It had a room opening off it that Father could use for a dressing room, and a private bath. She put Archie and Quentin in the room next to that, so that they would be close and she would hear them if they cried out in the night. There was one more room on that side of the hall, and I hoped it could be mine: it had a pretty bow window looking onto the garden. Mother and I looked out and admired the flowers.

"What's that?" she asked, pointing to a door in the room's side wall.

Father opened it. "A secret passageway," he said, giving Mother a wink, "to my office."

I looked inside. Father's office wasn't fancy, but it was full. His big desk was already covered with papers.

Mother smiled. "Then this room will be my library," she said. "My office. That way I can speak to you whenever I like."

She put Kermit in the room opposite the library. "You'll

40

share with Ted when he's at home," she said. She walked quickly down the far side of the hall, opening doors, talking to herself. Kermit and I ran ahead of her. There was an elevator, and beyond that a big room, nearly as large as Mother and Father's.

"This can be for me," I said. "Me and Sister. We'll share too."

Mother came in and looked it over. Like her office, it had a side door, which led into a long, narrow room next to it. "I think Sister had better have her own room," she said. "We'll give her this one. You can have the one next door, Ethel, the adjoining room. We'll use the tiny one for the housemaids and the leftover one for guests."

"That's not fair," Kermit said. His and Ted's room was smaller than Sister's.

"You'll be gone too," Mother said. "Sister won't be. Besides, she has more clothes than the rest of us put together."

My room was oddly shaped, long and very thin, because it had a bathroom stuck in one corner of it. The ceiling was so high that the room seemed narrower still. There were a brass bed in the corner by the door, an old bureau, some chairs, and a fireplace running down one long wall.

Sister's room had two brass beds, a big dark wooden bureau, and a dressing table. I liked her bureau better than mine. I ran my hand over the smooth top of the dressing table. I wished I were old enough to need one.

I wished I needed a big room. I wished I could do something to make them let me stay home.

"What about Miss Young?" I heard Kermit ask. He was

in the hall fiddling with the elevator. "What about Pinckney?"

I went out to the hall. Mother was shaking her head. Father said apologetically, "I've had some temporary rooms set up for them in the basement. There's room enough in the attic to throw together something a little nicer."

"Even then we'll have to assure them that it's only temporary," said Mother. "The attic for Pinckney! We'll have to get this second floor redone just as soon as possible." She pursed her lips at the glass door to the offices.

A porter brought my trunk up. "Which room, miss?"

I pointed. Father and I followed him in. "What do you think?" Father asked.

I went to the window. "You can't see the gardens," I said.

"No." He lifted me up. "You can see something better. See that building? That's the Navy Department. Do you remember? I used to work there."

I looked at the building, and I did remember. I had been six years old when Father was assistant secretary of the navy. He had rented a house for us in Washington, though we had sometimes stayed at Sagamore. One autumn day Mame had taken me to see Father in his office. I remembered standing on the steps looking up at the giant white building. It really was the same building I could see from my window.

"Remember when I came to visit you?" I said. "You bought us ices."

Father tweaked my nose. His eyes were smiling. "Lemon ices! That was a fine day."

Soon after that I'd gone back with Mother to Sagamore. Quentin was born. Then Father quit the navy to be a

42

Rough Rider in Cuba. Now for a moment I thought I could remember the taste of that lemon ice. "A fine day," I said, clutching Father's hand.

* * *

The next morning I woke up early. My pillow felt strange, and for a moment I had to blink and remember where I was. The Executive Mansion.

The sun was rising. I lifted the sash. Washington didn't smell half as bad as Mother said. There was a scent of horses, and gardens, and dampness. I looked down and saw carriages bumping through the streets, people hurrying along the walks. For the first time since Father became president, I felt a stirring of excitement. I thought of all the odd rooms in the mansion I hadn't had a chance to explore. I threw the bedroom door open and rushed out.

"Watch it!" Kermit yelled. *"Ethel!"* He was riding his bicycle down the hallway. He swerved hard to miss me and nearly fell over.

"No fair!" I said. "Where did you get your bicycle?" The last I had seen mine, it was being loaded onto the train.

"Pinckney has them," he said. "Downstairs."

"Get dressed first," Mother said, coming out of her room. "Always be dressed when you go downstairs. This is a public building; you never know whom you're going to meet." As I went back to my room to change out of my nightgown, Mother descended the staircase. I heard her say, "Good morning, Mr. Speaker. The president is not yet in his office."

Breakfast was served at 8:15, just like at home, and the

food tasted the same too, on account of our having brought our cook. Father was buoyant and laughing, and Mother smiled and joked with him. She went around the room throwing open the windows. "We must let some sunshine into the house," she said.

Father grinned. "You know, I think it *should* be thought of as a house," he said. "They've always called it the Executive Mansion, but that's not right, is it?"

Mother looked up at him, puzzled.

"It's the people's house," Father said. "It belongs to the people of the United States, not to the president who happens to be living in it. I'm going to have new stationery printed."

"Are you going to call it the People's House?" Kermit asked.

"No," said Father. "Too cumbersome. I'm going to call it the White House."

The White House. I liked it.

" 'S not very white," Kermit said, chewing a mouthful of eggs. "It's dark as a cave."

"The outside, silly," I said.

"We'll fix the inside, too, in time," Mother said. "I've already ordered flowers to be sent from the greenhouses, Theodore. I hope to unpack most of our books today. I've decided not to hire a housekeeper, but I think I really do need a social secretary."

A tall man came in. Father introduced him to us as Mr. Hoover, the chief usher. He was like a butler, Father said, only more important. "You two have a few days to explore,"

Father said to Kermit and me. "If you need to know where anything is, or if you need to know how anything works, ask Mr. Hoover."

Mr. Hoover smiled at us but seemed nervous. "Sir," he said, "shall I remove the rodent from the table?"

Father looked up. Kermit's rat was hopping toward the sugar bowl. "Oh, no," Father said. "It's the boy's pet. He's very tame."

"Very well, sir. And the kitten on the stairs?"

"That's Tom Quartz," I said. "He's not exactly tame."

"Shall I put him in the stables, sir?"

"Why, no," Father said. "He's the children's kitten. They'll tend to him." Mr. Hoover nodded and withdrew. "Hope he's not a nervous fellow," Father said. "He won't last long if he is."

Mother grinned. "I've asked Miss Young to bring Archie and Quentin on Thursday. Kermit, Ethel, your schools start next Monday."

I laid down my fork and lifted my chin. I tried to sound as much like Sister as possible. "I have decided," I said. "I'm not going. You can't make me."

"Dear Johnny," Father chuckled, "of course we can."

I hated being called Johnny. It was short for Elephant Johnny, Father's nickname for me when I was a baby. "Maybe I'll do something awful," I said.

"No, dear, of course you won't," Mother said serenely.

The horrible part was that she was right.

* * *

After breakfast Pinckney brought me my bicycle. Kermit and I ran races down the main-floor hallway until Mother came out and made rules. She said we were allowed to wear our stilts and ride our bicycles on the family side of the upstairs hallway, but we weren't to ride them downstairs. This was a shame, because the big rooms seemed made for bicycling. "Can we ride them outdoors?" I asked.

Mother looked surprised. "Of course," she said. "Anything you would do in the garden at Sagamore, you may do in the gardens here."

After that, I unpacked some of my things and took care of my rabbits and ran outdoors to the garden. Father and Mother were having guests to lunch, some senators, Mother said, and a Cabinet member or two, so Kermit and I were served luncheon in a smaller dining room. It was fun eating by ourselves. We grinned at each other across the table.

"Which Cabinet members were they?" Kermit asked. "Which senators?"

"I don't know," I said. "Mother didn't say. Do you know what any of them look like?"

Kermit shook his head. A few moments later Mr. Hoover came into the room. He addressed us formally. "Mr. Gilbert of the president's police would like to speak with you," he said.

"Us?" said Kermit.

Mr. Hoover nodded.

"Sure," I said.

I had already seen the policemen in their tall hats parading

46

the grounds that morning. I was glad of them. Now Mr. Gilbert came in and took an empty seat at the table. He removed his hat and shook hands with Kermit and me. "Now then," he said, "I'm the head of the police force here. Do you know what that means?"

"You try to keep Father safe," I said.

"Yes," he said. "We protect the president."

They hadn't done such a good job protecting President McKinley. I didn't say that out loud, but I exchanged looks with Kermit.

Mr. Gilbert sighed. "What happened to President McKinley must never be allowed to happen again," he said. "We will keep your father safe; we must do it. But that is why I want to talk to you. I want to enlist your help. Yours, and the older children's too, when they are home. I suppose you often go out riding with your father?"

We nodded. Father and Mother rode nearly every afternoon, and they liked us to come with them. Kermit was a strong rider, and I was a good one.

"If you are out with him on horseback, and a stranger rides at your father suddenly, I want you to spur your horse and get it in between your father and that stranger," Mr. Gilbert said.

I blinked. Kermit sat up straighter.

"I mean this," Mr. Gilbert said firmly. "A person trying to harm your father is not after Theodore Roosevelt. He is after the president of the United States. No one will try to hurt you. You must put yourselves in the way. Will you do that?"

47

"Yes," I said quickly.

"Yes," said Kermit. "Yes, of course we will."

"Good. Another thing. You must never let a man approach your father with his hands in his pockets, nor with a bandage on his hand or his arm in a sling. Not ever. If you see such a person coming near, you must shout or run at them or cause some kind of disturbance. Can you do that?"

"Yes," I said. "Of course we can."

"Of course," Kermit echoed. "Only—" He grinned. "If we make a big fuss and get into trouble with Mother, will you get us off the hook?"

Mr. Gilbert smiled solemnly. "Yes," he said. We shook hands all around on the deal, and he got up and left the room.

"That's good," Kermit said. "I'm glad the police are paying better attention now."

"About time," I said. I took another bite of my meat and chewed it slowly. "The only problem is, we're going to be stuck away in those stupid schools."

Kermit looked grim. "We'll be home on weekends," he said. "Anyway, they'll tell Archie and Quentin, too."

"Quentin can't stop an assassin. He's only three."

We were silent for a moment. I thought of Quentin hurling himself into a crowd of grown men. He would do it, I thought. He was bony, but he had plenty of energy. He would try.

"Archie can run him over with Algonquin," Kermit said. Then his face brightened. "And Mr. Gilbert will tell Sister. She'll be here most of the time. That'll help."

It would help, I was sure. Sister could fight like a wildcat. She was a match for anyone.

We ate for a few minutes without speaking. "One thing," Kermit said at last. "Don't tell Mother about any of this. She'd have Mr. Gilbert fired."

I nodded. Mother was at least as worried about Father as the rest of us, but I knew that what Kermit said was true.

Before she went to dinner, Mother read to Kermit and me in the library. She read to us for half an hour every day. "What would you like?" she asked.

"Sir Walter Scott," said Kermit.

Mother opened up a book called *The Pirate* and started at the beginning. It was a good book; I'd heard it before. I lay on my back on the sofa with my feet hanging over the arm and my head pressed against Mother's side. Her voice was so rhythmic and soothing that I was startled when she stopped reading and asked, "And which of you has been roller-skating in the East Room?"

Skating in circles while staring at the East Room ceiling was like looking through a kaleidoscope, only faster.

"That was me." It was how I'd spent the afternoon.

"Well, don't do it again," Mother said. "You've made marks all through the carpet."

"But I can't skate upstairs," I said. "The carpet in the hall is too thick."

"Then skate in the basement," Mother said.

"Yes, ma'am." I hadn't explored the basement yet. After Mother went to dinner, Kermit and I had a look.

You could get lost for a year down there. It was dark and dank and it seemed to go on forever, room after musty room connected by dim hallways lit with flickering gaslights. Pipes gurgled above our heads. Around one corner we found the kitchens, and our cook standing over the biggest stove we'd ever seen. "Cookies?" I asked.

He waved us away. "The president's invited extras for dinner again," he said. "No time for cookies today."

"We'll have parties down here," Kermit said as we skated away. "We'll get Father to tell us ghost stories and it'll be spooky as anything."

I skated after him, laughing. Father's ghost stories were the spookiest in the whole world, and the White House basement looked like a dungeon.

* * *

The next morning there was an article in the newspaper about my rabbits. I had taken them to the groundskeeper and arranged a place for their hutch, since rabbits prefer to live outdoors. The groundskeeper had been very nice about it. I couldn't believe he'd spoken to a newspaperman. "What do they mean, putting that in the paper?" I said.

"You're charming," Kermit said. "You're the president's wee daughter, and everyone wants to read about your bunnies."

"If they want to put one of us in the paper, it ought to be Sister," I said. "She'd like it."

"She'll get her chance, I'm sure." Father folded the newspaper and set it beside his plate. "Don't worry over it, Ethel. They can't do you any harm. But it's things like this that have us sending you to boarding school. The women in charge of the Cathedral School won't breathe a word about you to the press. It'll be nearly as discreet as Allenswood."

"Allenswood?" I said. "Please don't send me to Allenswood!" In all my worries, I'd never even thought of that. Allenswood was where Aunt Bamie and Aunt Corinne had gone to school. My cousin Eleanor was there at that moment. In England. An ocean away.

"Eleanor loves it there," Mother said.

"I can't go to Allenswood," I said. Tears sprang to my eyes. "I can't."

"Of course not, dear," Mother said soothingly. "We want you close to home."

Close to home, but not *at* home. "I shall never get used to school," I declared. "Never."

"Chin up," ordered Father.

I gulped. "Yes, Father."

* * *

Archie and Quentin arrived Thursday night. Mother and I went in the carriage to meet their train. Archie sat on Mother's lap the whole drive back, and Quentin sat on mine. They had brought the guinea pigs. Most of them were in a basket Miss Young carried, but Archie had one tucked into his blouse. "Careful, Mother, you'll squish

Bishop Doane," he said. Bishop Doane was the brown and white guinea pig.

"Let's put the poor creature back in the basket," Miss Young said.

"They like it when we carry them," said Archie.

"They do," I said. "We carry them in our shirts all the time at home."

Homesickness washed over me in a wave. In Albany or at Sagamore I could carry the guinea pigs around all day long, but if I did it here I would probably be in the newspaper, and I was sure I wouldn't be able to take guinea pigs to school. Or Tom Quartz. Or my bunnies. Or Wyoming. I wrapped my arms more tightly around Quentin and wished we were back at Sagamore.

The carriage turned the corner and we could see the White House ahead. "Look, boys," Mother said. "There it is."

Archie and Quentin scrambled to their feet. Quentin almost fell out of the carriage, but Miss Young caught him. She and Mother exchanged a sympathetic look. Then Mother patted my arm. "*This* is our home now," she said. "For at least the next three and a half years."

I blinked back tears. "Everything's so topsy-turvy," I said. Mother didn't answer, but the way she looked at me made me feel she understood.

* * *

"The National Cathedral School for Girls," Miss Young read to me that night, "in this, its first year of existence, has taken its stand among the foremost educational institutions for girls in America. Its graduates are admitted without entrance examinations to Mount Holyoke, Wellesley, Smith, and Vassar."

"I don't want to be admitted to Mount Holyoke, Wellesley, Smith, and Vassar," I said. "I don't even know what those things are. I told you, I want to stay home."

"And ride Wyoming in circles around your father," Miss Young said dryly. "Those are colleges, Ethel. For women."

"Ugh," I said. The last thing I wanted to do was go farther away.

"They give certificates, too, for those not wishing a full high school degree. Don't panic. There will be lots of different kinds of girls there."

On Friday morning Mother and Miss Young went through my clothes. I'd grown taller and stouter since the past winter. Mother made me try everything on while she and Miss Young poked and pinched me. "Too tight," Mother said, putting my old winter coat to one side. "Too short," she said about my good white dress.

"But that's my favorite!" I said. "I like that!"

"You can keep it here at home," Mother said. "It won't do for school."

School. "What do I have to wear at school?" I asked. Ted wore suits. Archie and Kermit wore regular boys' clothes.

"There's no uniform," Mother said. "You just need to be neatly dressed. You're a little girl, Ethel, they'll expect you to run and play."

I hoped so. I sat on the edge of my bed and watched

Mother count up the clothes in the "keep" pile and make shopping lists for Miss Young. "Remember," Mother said, "Ethel looks better in the sort of dress that doesn't have a waist."

I supposed the rest of the girls would look beautiful in tight-waisted dresses. They would be tall and willowy, like Sister. They'd probably laugh at my baby dresses. They'd sit elegantly in their elegant clothes and discuss whether they'd rather go to Mount Holyoke, Wellesley, Smith, or Vassar.

Not one would be homesick for a guinea pig. Not one would rather have a governess. Not one would be worrying about her father, the president.

Three new everyday dresses. One new good winter dress. A coat. Stockings, underwear. A good winter hat, and an everyday one. The shops in Washington were well stocked; shopping was easy. Miss Young smiled. "Having fun, dear?" she asked.

"No."

She squeezed my arm and bought me hair ribbons. I frowned over them. "Who will tie my ribbons when I'm at school?"

Miss Young looked thoughtful. "There must be a matron, someone in charge of the washing-up and things. Or you could ask one of the older girls to help you." I shuddered. "Tell you what," Miss Young said. "I believe you're old enough to manage your own hair ribbons. This afternoon I'll teach you how."

A warm flannel nightgown that touched the floor. A dressing gown to match. New slippers. Towels. "Why towels?" I said.

"The school says it provides bed and table linens and a

pair of blankets," Miss Young said, "but it doesn't say anything about towels."

"Don't we have towels at home I could bring?"

"Of course we do, Ethel, but wouldn't it be nice to start
school with new ones? Your bedspread from home, now,
that you should take with you."

"I will not!" I said. We had brought my bedspread from
Sagamore to put on my bed at the White House. I was not
moving it to school. "I'm keeping that at home," I said.

"But you'll want to make your room seem homelike."

"I will not," I said again, more loudly. "It won't *be*
home."

Overshoes. Gloves. A new hairbrush. Miss Young's list
was endless. She moved briskly from store to store. Shop-
keepers piled packages into our carriage. "One last stop,"
she said, smiling at me. She took me into a bookstore. It
smelled like new books, fresh and crisp.

"Schoolbooks." I sighed. "Do you have a list?" I hadn't
even asked what subjects I'd be studying.

"Oh, no," she said. "They'll give you those at the school.
Pick out something you'll enjoy, dear. You'll want something exciting to read during your free time."

"Really?" I said. Despite myself, I began to smile. I loved
books. "Do you think they'll really let us have free time?"

Miss Young laughed. "It's a school, Ethel, not a prison.
Of course they'll let you have free time! Now pick out a
book!"

I grinned. "Oh, thank you!"

I took so much time browsing through the shelves that

the storekeeper came to help me. "Here, miss," he said encouragingly, "lots of young ladies like *Little Lord Fauntleroy.*"

I giggled. "Father won't let us read that," I said.

The storekeeper looked affronted. "It's a very wholesome sort of book."

"Father said if any child of his ever acted like the namby-pamby fool in that book, he would throw it out into the woods to die." Father didn't mean that, of course, but he really had forbidden the book, and I wasn't about to make it my one treat for school.

The storekeeper blinked. "Louisa May Alcott?" he suggested.

"Oh, Mother doesn't allow us to read anything by *her.*" Mother hated Louisa May Alcott. I think Father secretly disagreed.

Suddenly I saw the perfect book: *Nicholas Nickleby.* I loved Charles Dickens. His books were full of excitement and adventure, and best of all, they were hundreds of pages long. I could read them for hours and hours and hours. Miss Young paid for the book, the clerk wrapped it in paper, and I carried it out under my arm. "Feel better, dear?" Miss Young asked.

I leaned against her. "Yes. Thank you."

* * *

On Monday school began. Archie left first. I thought Kermit envied him; I knew I did. Archie went to a regular public school right down the street, and he really did ride

58

Algonquin to get there. One of the doormen jogged beside him to make sure he did all right and to bring Algonquin home. After Archie had left, Mother took Kermit in the carriage. Miss Young was busy with Quentin, so I walked around the gardens and said good-bye to my favorite animals.

When Mother came back she said Kermit was going to be fine. "His school is very pleasant," she said. "I'm sure yours will be too." For a special treat she let me take my luncheon with her and Father. The secretary of the navy; Father's personal secretary, Mr. Loeb; and some other men were there too. Father always had lots of people to luncheon. They talked about trusts and monopolies and Panama and other things I didn't understand, so I didn't pay much attention. I ate my lunch politely and was careful not to cry. When Father got up—all the other men jumped up too—he kissed me gently on the cheek and whispered, "Do your best, Ethie. I'll see you on Friday."

I was glad Father had not forgotten I was leaving. Miss Young hugged me too, and Quentin let me kiss him, and then Mother and I climbed into the carriage and the coachman started the horses.

Four days before, the White House had seemed like a place where strangers lived. Now, as I drove away from it, it felt like home—or at least the closest thing to home nearby.

We drove through the city for what felt like forever, yet the ride took less time than I wanted it to. My heart was beating fast.

"What if I'm not smart enough?" I asked.

Mother patted me. "You are."

"How do you know? I've never studied with anyone but Sister."

She patted me again. "I know you," she said. "You'll do fine."

"What if I don't?" I asked. "Can I come home then?"

Mother stopped patting me and looked firm. "You may not," she said. "We expect you to do your best, Ethel, and if you do that, you cannot fail."

I nodded. I wouldn't fail. I wouldn't disappoint them.

The carriage entered a wood. The horses trotted over a stone bridge, their hooves making hollow noises. "There, Ethel," Mother said. "That's it. The big white building."

I gulped. The National Cathedral School went up and up and was square and wide. The copper roof sat on the stone bottom like a giant pointed hat. I supposed the White House was bigger, but it had Father in it, and Mother, and it seemed lower to the ground and more friendly. This building was not friendly at all.

"Isn't it lovely?" Mother said. "You'll enjoy being back here near the park. Away from crowds. Almost like Sagamore."

It wasn't at all like Sagamore.

"Miss Young can still teach me," I whispered.

"Ethel," Mother said firmly, "you must be brave. Think of your father, now."

Father hated cowards.

"Yes, ma'am," I whispered. We alighted from the carriage. I squared my shoulders and walked up the steps toward the huge wooden door.

There were girls everywhere, or so it seemed. Two carriages pulled in behind ours and had to wait while a porter helped our coachman unload my trunk. I heard squeals of laughter. In the entranceway two girls as big as Sister hugged each other with enthusiasm.

"Ahem." A woman pointedly cleared her throat. The two girls jumped to attention and bobbed their heads at her. "Good afternoon, Miss Bangs," they chorused. She nodded to them, then turned her attention to Mother and me.

"Miss Bangs," Mother said smoothly, "I am Edith Roosevelt. This is my daughter, Ethel. Ethel, meet Miss Bangs, one of the principals of your new school."

Miss Bangs shook Mother's hand. She smiled at me. Her smile looked as stony as the building.

I bobbed my head at her in imitation of the older girls. "Pleased to meet you, Miss Bangs," I said.

"I am pleased to meet you, Ethel," Miss Bangs said. "We've heard so much about you. I'm glad you will be joining our school."

Miss Bangs took us on a tour. She showed Mother the classrooms, the parlor, the dining hall, even the bathrooms and laundry. Everything was nearly new and very clean, with a plainness that made me long for the ornate, gloomy old White House. Miss Bangs spoke to Mother as we walked. "There are nearly fifty girls enrolled in the school this year," she said. "Two-thirds of them are boarders. We graduated two girls last spring." Miss Bangs looked down at me. "You'll be one of the younger students, but there are a few others your age." She looked back at Mother. "And your older girl?" she asked expectantly.

Mother hesitated. "Alice is staying with family in Connecticut right now," she said.

"She's not coming," I said. "She says she won't." I sounded petulant even to myself. I was sorry for it.

Miss Bangs pursed her lips. "We would welcome her later, of course," she said.

"Of course," Mother said.

We climbed one flight of stairs, then another. "We're very pleased with our dormitory situation," Miss Bangs said. "Ethel, here is your room."

It was bare and clean with a polished wood floor. The iron bed had been made up with white sheets and the promised pair of blankets, and there were an empty closet, a desk, a plain bookshelf, and a small shining porcelain washstand. A high window let in plenty of light but no warmth; the furniture was stiff and functional and the room felt cold.

Mother looked around. "Very neat," she said slowly.

I had peeked into some of the other girls' rooms as we'd walked past. They had warm rugs, bright spreads, and tasseled curtains. We could hear girls nailing pictures to their walls.

I had only my clothes and my new towels and a copy of *Nicholas Nickleby*. I hadn't even brought my own pillow, and the bed didn't have one. I hadn't thought about pillows. I hadn't thought how empty my room would be.

Miss Bangs said she would expect me in the assembly room at three o'clock. She shook hands with Mother and left us alone.

Mother patted my shoulder. "Not very cozy, is it?" she said. "I'm sorry, but never mind. It's only for this week. I'll ask Miss Young to look for a nice rug for you, and we'll get you some curtains. We'll make it better."

I wished I had a roommate. I wished Sister were there.

Mother sat down on the bed and drew me to her. "Don't look so woebegone. It's a fine school. The girls seem friendly. You'll be happy here. I'm sorry about the room. I didn't think. You know"—she smothered a little laugh into my hair—"the problem with the Executive Mansion is that it has too much decoration."

"The White House," I whispered.

"Yes." She stood up and smoothed her skirt. "I need to

go now. Hang up your dresses and set everything out just as you like it. I'll send a carriage for you the instant classes are over on Friday afternoon. I promise."

Mother always kept her promises.

She kissed me and went out, softly closing the door of my room. I imagined her graciously sweeping down the flights of stairs, out to the waiting carriage. I imagined the coachman helping her inside, tipping his hat to her, closing the door. I imagined the carriage pulling away, the horses clip-clopping over the stone bridge.

I would not cry. I would not. I thought of Father, how he had always wished he were strong enough to go to school when he was a boy. I thought of Ted gritting his teeth and setting off for Groton without even Mother to go with him. I thought of Kermit's calm face that morning as the carriage took him away.

I could be as brave as any boy, as strong as any of my brothers. I opened my trunk and began to unpack.

We assembled at three o'clock. The hall clock began to chime and I scrambled down the steps with the other girls and tried to act as if I belonged. I found a seat near some girls who looked almost as young as me. One of them smiled at me. I smiled back. There seemed to be dozens of students, but we only half filled the large assembly room.

My new shoes hurt and my stocking had bunched under one heel. I squirmed to set it straight. One of the teachers tapped me on the shoulder as she marched past me down the aisle. "Sit up," she commanded. Someone giggled.

The teacher who had tapped me was Miss Whiton, the other principal. The first thing she told us, after her name, was that she had a bachelor's degree from Smith College, one of the places Miss Young had told me about. I'd never known a woman who'd gone to college before. Mother hadn't, nor Aunt Bamie, nor Miss Young. It didn't make me like Miss Whiton any better.

Miss Bangs and Miss Whiton introduced the rest of the teachers: Miss Marshall, who taught the primary class; Miss

Greaves, who ran the library; and Miss Stapleton, who taught physical education. I looked at Miss Stapleton with some interest. She spoke of the school's new tennis courts, and I grinned. I hadn't known we'd be allowed to play outside, and I adored tennis. We played it on the lawn at Sagamore.

Father loved tennis too, but he wasn't very good at it. He liked to think he was, though. He said he was going to have a tennis court put in on the lawn of the White House.

While I was thinking about Father and tennis, Miss Whiton kept on introducing teachers. The French and German teachers spoke with accents. I didn't know a word in either language. Father did; he spoke both fluently. He could speak Italian, too. He'd lived in Dresden for a winter when he was small. Sometimes when he and Aunt Bamie or Aunt Corinne didn't want my brothers and cousins and me to understand what they were saying, they spoke in German or French.

Suddenly all the girls were on their feet, singing a song I didn't know. I jumped up and pretended to mouth the words. The teachers paraded out of the room. We hurried out behind them.

"Where are we going?" I asked the girl beside me.

She gave me a strange look. "Weren't you listening?"

"No."

"We can play outside until it's time for dinner."

"What are we going to play?"

"I'm riding my bicycle. I don't know what you're going to do."

I watched in envy as nearly all the girls my age rushed off in a pack to the bicycle shed. The school was surrounded by open land and there was plenty of room.

I went up to Miss Bangs, who was surveying the scene. "I didn't know we could bring bicycles," I said. "Are there any extras?"

"Didn't you read your handbook?" Miss Bangs asked.

I shook my head. I'd thrown it in the garbage bin.

"We don't supply bicycles," she said. "Bring your own next week. I understand you won't be boarding with us on the weekends." She sounded as though she disapproved.

"No, ma'am."

"Do you play tennis, Ethel?"

"I didn't bring my racquet."

"The school keeps a supply of tennis racquets," she said. "We have a wide variety of equipment designed for exercise. Regular physical activity promotes health, you know. We find it an important component of the well-being of our girls."

She talked to me as though she were still talking to Mother. I stared at her.

Miss Bangs sighed. "Go run, Ethel," she said. "If you don't know what to do with yourself, run around the yard."

So I ran, even though my shoes hurt my feet. I'd made it halfway around the lawn when one of the girls caught up to me. I started to smile at her, but she said, "Chatting up Miss Bangs already, are we? I suppose you think you're too important for the rest of us."

* * *

At dinnertime we descended to the dining room on the lower floor. Wide windows looked out onto a lawn dotted with young trees. The room was elegant, the tables set with white cloths and silver. Along one end was a dais where the principals sat at their own table. We were made to march past it in two lines before we sat down.

Tables were assigned; Miss Mallett, the science teacher, presided at mine. There were eight other girls, and they all looked older than me and more prepared. I felt like the only new girl.

I reached for my napkin. "Not yet," Miss Mallett murmured. I snatched my hand back. We bowed our heads while, at the podium, the religion teacher read a Bible verse and said grace. When she said "Amen" we were allowed to move.

The food smelled good, and I was hungry. I put my napkin on my lap, picked my fork up carefully, and began to eat.

Miss Mallett started the conversation the way Mother might when she had a table full of strangers at a dinner. "Harriet, here," she said, indicating a willowy dark-haired girl beside her, "will be a member of our second graduating class this spring. She intends to earn a classical diploma."

We all looked at Harriet, who looked back proudly. I didn't know what a classical diploma was. Probably something that got you into Mount Holyoke, Wellesley, Smith, or Vassar.

"And little Ethel," said Miss Mallett, "is President Roosevelt's daughter."

Heads swiveled in my direction. Eyes opened wide. Harriet snorted. "*You're* the president's daughter?" she said. "But you're nothing but a child! Everyone said you were *sophisticated*!"

"Harriet," Miss Mallett warned.

"But they *did*," Harriet said, "and she can't be out of the primary class."

"That's the other one, Harriet—the older one," a different girl said. "This isn't the girl from the newspapers."

"Yes, I am," I said. I wasn't happy about being in the newspapers, but I was determined to be honest. Father valued honesty. "It was me they put in about the rabbits."

This caused a gale of laughter that I didn't understand. Even Miss Mallett smiled.

"I certainly wasn't asking about your *rabbits*," said Harriet with a sniff. "We've read all about the fashionable Miss Roosevelt, who goes to parties and dances and does nothing but have fun." Harriet, the classical scholar, sounded envious.

"That's Sister," I said. Oh, how I wished she were there! Sister wouldn't let them laugh at me. Sister would know what to say. I twisted my napkin in my lap.

"Your sister—yes. What's her name?"

"Alice. But we call her Sister. She's seventeen."

"And she's your half sister, correct? Didn't I read something about that?" Harriet's eyes glittered. They made me squirm.

"She's my sister," I said. "That's all."

Miss Mallett changed the subject. The girls began to

talk of the National Zoo being established at Rock Creek Park. The school was planning an excursion there the following Saturday.

"Father loves the National Zoo," I said. "He thinks that the more regular people get to see wild animals, the more they'll understand why we need to preserve open land out west. But I won't be able to go on the school trip. I go home Friday afternoon." I smiled at Miss Mallett.

"*Regular* people?" retorted Gertrude, the tall girl to Harriet's left. "Don't the Roosevelts consider themselves regular people?"

A smaller girl named Emily who sat across the table said, in a voice that was practically a wail, "They wouldn't let *me* spend weekends at home!"

"Well," Harriet said with a malicious grin, "you must be one of the regular people, that's why."

"Girls!" said Miss Mallett.

"I—I didn't mean it that way," I said. "I meant people who don't get to travel and see animals living in the wild. I never have." Mother and Sister and Ted had been to Father's land out west, but I hadn't. "I don't know why I'm allowed to go home on Fridays," I said. "I just am." *Thank goodness.*

Across the table, Emily wiped her eyes on her napkin. She looked about my age. I wanted to tell her that I understood how she felt, that I was homesick too, but I'd already talked myself into enough trouble. I bowed my head and kept quiet.

All the next morning we took test after test, so that the teachers could see where we belonged in our classes. Butterflies floated in my stomach. Miss Young had never tested Sister and me. She said she knew what we were learning without exams. But what if I was stupider than all the other girls?

We sat at individual desks, with ink and pens, while the teachers put papers in front of us and told us how long we had to complete them. The clock ticked anxiously. When the time was up, one teacher collected papers while another handed out more. History, science, grammar, mathematics. Foreign languages I didn't know a word of. My head ached. My legs didn't quite reach the floor, and they ached too.

Around ten-thirty we were given a glass of milk and allowed to move about for ten minutes. I stood and stretched. There were ten girls in the classroom with me, including Emily. I tried to catch her eye, but she looked away.

Soon a teacher came in and told us to sit down again. I wiped my sweaty hands on my skirt. We were given compositions to write. I loved writing. In my family, we wrote letters all the time, and Miss Young often assigned me compositions. I settled into my seat, feeling more comfortable. Surely I couldn't fail everything.

At lunch I was too hungry to talk. Miss Mallett carried on conversations with some of the girls who hadn't spoken much the night before. I saw that we were all expected to contribute.

Emily said her father was a minister. She had two younger sisters. This was her first time away from home. Her lip trembled a bit as she said it.

"What sort of activities do you enjoy?" Miss Mallett asked. "What opportunities do you hope to take advantage of here this year?"

That was just the sort of question a teacher would ask. Not are you homesick, do you miss your mother or your dogs or your pesky brothers. Opportunities and advantages, as though being at school were a gift.

But Emily's face lighted into a smile. "I'm going to learn to play the piano," she said. "Mother said I might. And Father said we'd be able to explore all over the city."

Miss Mallett smiled approvingly. We were all supposed to say we were glad to be there.

In the afternoon we had free time, but it was raining and we couldn't play outdoors. The dormitory floor was filled with the noise of girls visiting and laughing and slamming doors. I was used to commotion—I had to be, with Quentin and Archie around—but I wasn't used to so many strangers. I shut myself inside my room. First I wrote a long letter to Sister. Then I wrote a letter to Kermit, and one to Ted. Then I read *Nicholas Nickleby* until supper-time.

The class assignments were posted in the hall outside the dining room. I searched nervously down the lists for my name. I hadn't failed the exams. I'd even passed into the third class of English. I already knew the work of the first two years, Hawthorne, Longfellow, Irving, Lowell. Those were authors Father and Mother liked to read to us. I had received high marks for my composition.

In the rest of my classes I stayed with the first year, which I guessed was all right, since it was where most of the ten-year-olds were assigned. Ted was a year behind his age group at Groton, because of being sick when he was small, and Father didn't like that. I hoped he'd be satisfied with my position.

I would learn Latin. Greek. French. German. The history and geography of the United States. That seemed easy; Father was always telling us stories about the past. Botany. Zoology. Old Testament history. Christian ethics. Grammar school arithmetic and concrete geometry. It seemed like a lot of work. Then I had two pleasant surprises. Mother had signed me up for singing classes twice a week, and I was to learn to play the piano, like Emily.

I wondered if the White House had a piano. I'd have to look when I got home.

The school offered riding lessons too, but Mother hadn't signed me up for them, I supposed since I already knew how to ride. It would have been lovely, though, to spend a few extra hours each week on the back of a horse. I was always happy when I was riding.

* * *

When classes started Wednesday they weren't as awful as I'd feared. I could understand the work and keep up, and some of the girls in the first prep year seemed nice. But none of them, not even Emily, approached me or acted as if she wanted to be my friend. The little primary students giggled when they saw me, and the older girls pretended I didn't exist. On Thursday at supper Miss Mallett said, "Your young brothers were in the newspaper this morning, Ethel. Seems they were flooding the backyard of the mansion with a garden hose in an attempt to stage a naval battle."

I grinned. "They were probably acting out the attack on the *Maine* from the War of 1812," I said. "That's their favorite." Father was always telling us naval stories about the War of 1812; he'd even written a book about it. Uncle Will said the book was so good, the naval academy used it as a textbook.

Harriet sniffed. "I would think that someone would prevent them from such destructiveness. That lawn is government property."

"I'm sure Archie and Quentin didn't destroy anything," I said. "Naval battles never hurt the lawn at Sagamore." That was a lie. The last time Archie had engineered a flood it had taken the gardeners weeks to repair the grass. But I wasn't going to admit that to Harriet, who seemed to want to dislike me. "We have to have somewhere to play," I said.

"I hear you use the East Room," said Gertrude. "That was in the newspapers too."

I hated newspapers. How did they hear about me and the East Room? "I said I'd stay in the basement from now on."

"The story wasn't about you," Miss Mallett said smoothly, over giggles from the other girls. "I believe there were some potted palms in some seats there? Apparently they've been removed, and your brothers are using the spaces for hiding places."

I was glad Mother had removed those dreadful palms, but I hated the idea of Archie and Quentin having fun without me. When I got home, we'd have to have a long game of hide-and-seek.

"The East Room isn't in very good shape," I said carefully. "I don't think Archie and Quentin could hurt it. We're going to redo it as soon as Congress approves."

Harriet sniffed. "It was good enough for President McKinley," she said.

I bit my lip. I hated to even think of poor President McKinley. What if Father's plans were cut short the same way?

"Can't the children be confined to a playroom?" Miss Mallett asked me.

How should I know? I thought. *I'm not their governess.* And it wasn't as though we had any extra rooms upstairs. But I could just see where that conversation would go. If I said the White House wasn't big enough, they'd all think I was a spoiled brat. Never mind that we had eight people and only five bedrooms.

"Please pass the potatoes," I said.

Friday came and my week was over at last. Just as Mother had promised, the White House carriage was waiting when I flew out the door. The horses were unfamiliar, but I knew the coachman. His name was Arthur; he often drove Father. "Can I ride up with you?" I asked him.

"Sure, Miss Ethel." He gave me a hand. I looked over my shoulder. Wouldn't Miss Whiton have a fit if she saw me! I doubted Cathedral School girls were supposed to sit on the carriage box.

"No luggage?" he asked.

"Just my book bag." I had it over my shoulder. "The school does our laundry. I'm bringing my bicycle on Monday, and my tennis racquet." And I had a list for Miss Young: gym uniforms, to be bought at a particular store in Washington; special pencils for drawing class; a pair of shoes suitable for indoor exercise.

He started the horses. The harness jangled as we drove away. I breathed deeply. "I'm so glad to be going home, Arthur."

"You don't care for that school?" He glanced back.

"Looks like a pretty fancy place to me. And kind of nice the way it's set back in the woods."

"It looks all right, I guess," I said, "but I hate it. I'm not going to talk about it. I'm not going to talk about anything unpleasant all weekend. What are the boys up to? And whose horses are these?"

Arthur chuckled. "Those rascal brothers of yours are up to every bit of no-good in this world. Last I saw them, they were watering the sandbox, having been expressly forbidden to continue watering the lawn. The horses are a new pair the president bought on Tuesday. Easy steppers. Like them?"

I did. I watched their glossy hindquarters sway as they trotted down the road. "Can't they go faster?" I asked.

"Not on these cobblestones. Can't wreck the carriage, Miss Ethel."

I sighed. "Has Sister written this week? Is she still at Aunt Bamie's house? How's Ted? Does Kermit like his school?" I felt as if everything could have changed in the five days I'd been gone.

"I don't know any of that, Miss Ethel. Don't fret. You'll be home in ten minutes."

I watched the horses longingly. "Can I drive them?" I loved to drive. I had learned at Sagamore with Pony Grant and our pony trap. Mame had always let me. But I had never driven such beautiful horses.

Arthur grinned and passed me the reins. "So long as you promise not to go too fast," he said, "and let me have them back before anyone from home can see."

Arthur watched me carefully, but only once, when we

77

were passed by a four-in-hand, did he have to put his hands over mine.

"Well done, Miss Ethel," he said, taking over again as the White House came into view. "You drive a treat."

"Oh, thank you!" Already I felt so much better. And now I was home!

Arthur pulled the carriage around to the stables, not the White House door. "Something in here the president wants you to see."

"Oh, what is it?" I hopped down from the box unassisted and ran into the stables. "Father? It's me!"

"Ethel!" He picked me up and swung me around. "I'm so glad to see you! How are you?"

"Miserable," I said promptly. "I don't like—"

He grinned. "You look splendid!"

"That's only because—"

He cut my words off. "Look here!" He caught my hand, led me to one of the box stalls, and lifted me up so that I could see through the grate. Inside, a tall, handsome bay horse stood ankle deep in bright new straw. He looked at us warily. "What do you think?"

"He's beautiful! Is he ours?"

"You bet he's ours!" Father grinned so hard he looked ready to burst. "Just arrived today. He's a present from Mr. George Bleistein—a jumping horse from the Geneseo Valley. By Jiminy! It's worth being president, most of the time. I can't wait to try him!"

I laughed. "What's his name, Father?"

"I don't suppose he has one yet." Father looked at me.

"We'll call him Bleistein, won't we, after Mr. Bleistein. Bleistein! Here, boy!" Father fed the horse some sugar he took from the pocket of his frock coat. He poured some into my hands so that I could feed Bleistein too. The horse's muzzle was warm and slobbery.

Father and I skipped arm in arm back to the main house. "Your mother's receiving callers in the Blue Room," he said. He checked his watch as we went through the main door. "Should be done any minute. You'll want to meet this new secretary she's—"

"*Boo!*" Quentin jumped up from one of the potted-palm seats. They really were great hiding places; we were caught completely by surprise. I screeched, and Father jumped.

"Quentin!" Father yelled. "How many times have I told you—"

"You're a bear!" Quentin shouted. "Ahhh!" He leapt onto Father's shoulders.

"Grrr!" Father said. "A big bear, a great big grizzly bear, going to eat you up!" He pretended to gobble Quentin's leg.

"Help!" yelled Quentin.

"I'll save you!" I launched myself onto Father's back.

"No, I'll save him!" Archie came running from a corner somewhere, wearing his Rough Riders costume and carrying a bow and arrow. He dropped his weapons and tackled Father's legs.

"Grrwl! Grr! The bear refuses to yield! The bear will not go down!" Father shook his head and shoulders. He lumbered down the hall like a great grizzly. "The bear is a mighty hunter!" He shook Quentin upside down. Quentin howled with laughter. Archie and I hung on to his arms. Father dragged me along.

"The bear begins to weaken," Father said. He sank to his knees. "The mighty beast cannot be vanquished, but the determined hunters bring him"—Archie broke free, took a flying leap, and tackled Father's head—"down," said Father. "Archiekins, I hope you haven't broken my spectacles again."

"Good afternoon, Mr. President." A calm voice interrupted us. I looked up. A sad-looking old man in mourning clothes stood before us with his hat in his hand.

Father shook Archie off and shifted Quentin to the carpet. He sat up. His frock coat was rumpled, his shirt untucked below his vest, his hair and spectacles askew. Father smiled. "Good afternoon, John," he said quietly. "Good to see you. Ethel, dear, shake hands. I don't believe you've ever met Mr. Hay. He was President McKinley's secretary of state, and he has agreed to continue as mine."

I stood up, smoothed my skirt, and shook Mr. Hay's offered hand. Even when Father had been governor I had heard him speak admiringly of Mr. Hay. "Are you the man who worked for President Lincoln, sir?"

He made a slight bow. "Yes, Miss Ethel. I had the honor of being his personal secretary. Mr. President, I will wait in your office." I watched him as he headed toward the stairs.

"He's so sad," I said. "Did he love President McKinley?"

Father got to his feet. He put his hand on my shoulder. "He did, but it's worse than that. His own son died recently."

He patted me. "Go find your mother now. Take these mighty hunters with you."

I grabbed Quentin's hand. "I'm home!" I said. Archie war-whooped, and the three of us ran toward the stairs. "I'm home!"

Saturday morning Quentin ran down the wide main-floor hallway. "Tom Pen, Tom Pen!" he yelled. "One of the guinea pigs had babies, and I didn't even know he was a girl!" He came back down the hallway tugging on the arm of a tall, bearded old man, the doorkeeper I'd seen on our first night. "Come look!" he said.

The old man grinned and lifted Quentin to his shoulders. "Guinea pig babies!" he said. "Well, which one was it?"

"Bishop Doane! My favorite!" Quentin giggled.

I went upstairs with them and looked at the guinea pigs in their box in the boys' bedroom. Bishop Doane was surrounded by a litter of tiny mewling piglets. "You'll want a separate box for her now," I said.

"That you will," agreed the doorman.

"Ethel, do you know Tom Pen?" Quentin demanded. "He's my best friend after Mr. Craig." Mr. Craig was one of the White House policemen. Quentin adored him.

"No, sir." I shook the man's hand. "Ethel Roosevelt."

"Thomas Pendel," he said.

"Pleased to meet you, Mr. Pendel."

He shook his head. "Call me Tom Pen," he said. "Children always call me Tom Pen."

Quentin hung on the man's trousers. "Tad Lincoln called him that," he said. "Tom Pen was doorman for his father too. Tell her, Tom Pen."

Tom Pen's face brightened. "It's true. I've been here ever since Lincoln took office, forty years ago. I loved that little Tad. All these years since, there's never been the same kind of liveliness in this house—until now." He ruffled Quentin's hair and smiled.

* * *

"Did everybody here work for President Lincoln first?" I asked Father when he came in before lunch.

"No, of course not," he said. "Why do you ask?"

I told him about Tom Pen. "And Mr. Hay," I said.

"They're old men, both of them," Father said. "I didn't know Tom Pendel had been here that long." He paused thoughtfully. "I'm surprised, really, that there's anyone left here who remembers Lincoln. I saw his funeral procession in New York, you know, when I was just a little boy. It's very nearly the first thing I can remember." Mother came into the room, and Father looked up at her and smiled. "And your mother was there too. We were looking out the second-story windows of my grandfather's old house. But she started to cry, and her nurse had to take her away."

"Pshaw," Mother said.

I knew President Lincoln was Father's hero, the greatest president, Father once said, who had ever lived. "Lincoln was assassinated," I said, then covered my mouth with my hands. I hadn't meant to blurt that out.

A flicker of worry passed over Mother's face, but Father only laughed. "A man can't spend his life looking over his shoulder!" he said. "I'm sure Lincoln would have said the same thing."

Lincoln might have, I thought. *But not Lincoln's family.*

* * *

Father and Mother tried to go for a ride every afternoon. Saturday we all went, except Quentin, of course: Mother on her mare, Yagenka; me on Wyoming, the only horse we had besides Yagenka and old Diamond that could carry a sidesaddle; Kermit on Renown; Archie on Algonquin; and Father on the new horse, Bleistein. Kermit sat very tall. I could tell he was proud of being put up on Renown, who had been Father's best hunter before Bleistein arrived. The stirrup leathers on Renown's saddle were too long, so Father had Kermit put his feet through them, resting on top of the stirrups instead of inside them.

"Really," Mother said, "someone could punch holes in those leathers."

"I'm fine like this," Kermit said. "I am." He turned Renown in a careful circle. His eyes shone.

"If you get along with him," Father said, "we'll get a saddle for him that fits you."

Mr. Gilbert, one of the policemen, led two saddled

horses out of the stable. Mr. Craig came up and took one of them. The crease in Mother's forehead smoothed. "How lovely that you could join us," she said.

Father scowled. "A simple ride with my family—"

"These horses need exercise something desperate, sir," said Mr. Gilbert.

"We were hoping to watch how that new one goes," said Mr. Craig.

"Oh, very well." Father fussed with his crop and gloves. "All this following about is simply ridiculous. Still"— he looked down at Bleistein fondly—"can't blame you. Let's go!"

I had learned to ride astride on Algonquin when I was very small, but Mother had made me switch to sidesaddle after a year. She thought it was immodest for girls to ride astride. Father disagreed. "All the young ladies out west ride astride," he often said. "A split skirt is no more revealing than a riding habit. Furthermore, it's a darned sight safer to have one leg on each side of the horse, with no great big sidesaddle horn to get caught on when you fall. I do wish you'd reconsider, Edie."

Mother never reconsidered. So I sat high up on Wyoming, my left foot in a stirrup, my right knee crossed in front of me over the saddle horn, my skirt flapping in the wind. Wyoming didn't mind. Neither did I. I was used to sidesaddle, and anyway, that was how Mother rode.

Bleistein surged to the front of our group. I put Wyoming into a canter and sailed after him. Soon we were all galloping, Kermit looking pale but resolute, keeping a firm hand on Renown, Mother laughing and urging Yagenka onward. "Whoopee!" yelled Archie, far in the rear. Algonquin did his best, but his pony legs were so much shorter than the horses' that he could never keep up. Mr. Gilbert hung back with him. Mr. Craig rode up front.

Bleistein got his head down and let off a series of terrific bucks, *wham! wham!*, his heels flying as high as Father's hat. Father laughed and spurred him forward. Bleistein shot ahead, then tried to buck again, but this time Father held him.

"He's a good one!" Father yelled. "He's a keeper!"

I grinned. Father really was a cowboy. He could ride anything.

We rode all through Rock Creek Park. I thought about the girls' going on a field trip to the zoo there. As we trotted closer to the school, I told Kermit about it. "They all look at me funny, because I'm the president's daughter," I said. "It's like they expect something from me. I think they're waiting for reasons to hate me. You should hear the questions they ask me. Why is Father keeping President McKinley's Cabinet? Why is Quentin allowed to parade with the policemen? Why hasn't Sister come home?

"Even if I knew the answers," I said, smacking Wyoming with my crop so that he'd keep up with Renown, "I'm learning I shouldn't tell them. Whatever I say upsets somebody."

"You've only been there a week," Kermit said. "Give them a chance to get used to you. You don't even know yourself what it's like yet to be the president's daughter."

I wanted to say that I was not any different. I was the same daughter and Father was the same father as we were before President McKinley died. "People didn't act like this in Albany," I said, "and I was the governor's daughter there."

Kermit sighed in exasperation. "First of all, there are forty-five governors in the United States. There's only one president. Second, you didn't go to school in Albany. School's always different."

"What's your school like, then?"

"It's all right," he said. "The teachers are good. I like my classes. The dormitory's awful crowded, and they keep us so busy we never have a spare moment to think."

I nodded.

"Once I pretended to take longer over my homework than I needed to, just so I could be quiet for a few minutes more," he continued. "And I wrote to Ted twice. They like it when we write letters. They give us time to do that."

"I wrote Sister," I said. "I told her the Cathedral School was the most fun place I had ever been, and that I was sorry she was missing out on such a good time."

Kermit snorted. "Did you really?"

I grinned. "Yes. But she won't believe me."

"If she went to that school," Kermit said, "from all the things you've told me, she'd last about a week."

I thought of Miss Bangs and the way she held her mouth when something displeased her. "I don't think she'd last even that long."

On Monday Arthur drove the carriage much too fast. I wanted to ask him to slow down, please, but Miss Young had put me into the carriage with my bicycle and racquet and parcels, and I couldn't climb out while we were moving. In no time at all we were there. Arthur helped me unload.

"Hurry, Ethel," Miss Bangs called. "Classes begin in fifteen minutes."

I hurried. I wheeled my bicycle to the shed and ran to put my book bag and parcels in my room. I had to make three trips, because one of the parcels was a rug wrapped around my tennis racquet, and another was a bedspread and pillow. I didn't unpack at all, just threw everything onto my bed and ran back downstairs.

I was late anyway. The last girl into the classroom. It was English, the class I had with the twelve-year-olds. As they looked at me I felt my face turn red. Miss Whiton looked grim. "If you continue to go home on weekends, Ethel, you must endeavor to return on time."

"Yes, ma'am."

"Coming in late disrupts the others."

"Yes, ma'am."

"I hope you've finished your assigned reading."

"Yes, ma'am."

"Sit down."

I sat.

Right at that moment Father and Mother would be taking their walk through the rose gardens before Father started work. Quentin and Miss Young would be watching the White House policemen on their morning drill. Archie would be riding Algonquin down the street to school. Kermit and Ted would be hunched over desks like mine, only Kermit would be happier, because he didn't mind school, much, and Ted would be more miserable, because he did. At Aunt Bamie's house Sister would still be asleep, I was sure, and when she did wake up her maid would bring breakfast to her room on a tray. Aunt Bamie was a great believer in breakfast on trays.

"Ethel, are you paying attention?"

I jumped. More giggles.

* * *

I had forgotten to do my Latin homework. I hadn't practiced my piano exercises either, because the piano at the White House hadn't been used for so long that it was completely out of tune. "That shouldn't have kept you from practicing," the piano teacher said severely.

"Mother and Father were hosting a dinner," I said,

looking at the floor. "The piano's on the main floor. The noise was disruptive, so Mother asked me to stop."

The teacher rapped her pencil on the music rack of the school piano. "And this dinner, it lasted the *entire* weekend? There wasn't a free half hour?"

I'd had to hug Quentin, and listen to Mother's stories, and cuddle both the new guinea pigs and the old ones. I'd had to play tennis with Kermit and ride Wyoming through the park. I'd had to go to church with Mother and Kermit. I'd had to do all the things I couldn't do while I was at school, but I didn't think the teacher would understand that. The only time I could have spared for piano was when Father and Mother were at dinner and Miss Young was putting the little boys to bed.

"I'm sorry," I said.

"I expect you to do better next weekend. It's no use taking lessons if you don't practice."

By lunchtime I was more homesick than ever. We were served great hot slices of roast beef—the food at school was always good—but I couldn't figure out how to swallow it past the lump in my throat. I sipped my milk and rearranged my peas. I wasn't hungry.

Emily looked at me shyly. "Did you have a nice weekend?" she asked.

Tears welled up in my eyes and for one horrid moment I thought I was really going to cry. Once I started, I wouldn't be able to stop. I thought how Harriet would laugh to see me blubbering. I thought how ashamed Father would be. I swallowed hard. "I don't want to talk about it," I said.

Emily looked bewildered, as though I'd meant the words to hurt her. I hadn't, of course.

"I guess your family isn't as cozy as they say in the papers," Harriet observed.

"You can't believe everything you read in the papers," I said, because it was true.

* * *

I felt as if I'd been split into two people, Home Ethel, who was cheerful and happy and could do many things well, and School Ethel, who never stood a chance. Whatever I said came out wrong. Whatever I did wasn't quite right. That night I shut the door of my room hard and wrote a long letter to Sister. I told her everything. First I wrote about school and Emily and the other girls and how lonely I was and how hard it was to fit in. Then I told her about living in the White House. I told her about Bleistein, and Kermit riding Renown. I told her how all the dogs were doing. I told her about Lincoln and Tom Pen.

Sister didn't like to be serious, so I expected her to ignore the first part of the letter and only answer the part about the dogs and horses. I was wrong. I got a letter from her at lunchtime on Friday, the only bright spot in a horrible week.

She didn't have any advice for me, she said. But she wrote that she knew exactly how I felt. She said sometimes she was lonely too.

Sister had never said she was lonely before. I was certain it was true.

She'd signed the letter, *Love, Sister*. I tucked it into my dress pocket and took it upstairs. I brought all my other letters home on Fridays, but this one I would keep at school. I would use it to remind myself that I was not entirely alone.

I had met Mother's new secretary, Belle Hagner, the weekend before. She was young and pretty and I liked her very much. On Friday when I got home from school, Mother and Belle were sitting together in Mother's library, frowning over a piece of paper. Mother kissed me when I rushed in.

"What's wrong?" I asked. I hugged her and kissed her again.

Belle looked worried. Mother cuddled me and smiled. "Newspapers," Mother said.

"Clothes," said Belle. "Your mother's clothes are important news now. The reporters all want descriptions of everything she wears. Tonight is another state dinner—"

"Not a formal one yet, of course," Mother said. We were all still in official mourning for President McKinley and would be until the New Year's reception. "But a state dinner nonetheless. I'm wearing my blue gown."

I snuggled next to her. "I like your blue gown."

"I do too," said Mother. "But I wore it to a dinner last

week, and the week before that. And I'll have to wear it again next week." She sighed. "I only have four evening gowns. Can't we label them A, B, C, and D? We can send out sketches to the press, with color descriptions, and afterward just tell them, 'Tonight Mrs. Roosevelt will be wearing gown C.' "

I could tell that Mother thought the whole thing was funny. Miss Hagner seemed amused but anxious. "We have to tell them something," she said.

"I will order a few more gowns soon," Mother said. "But I'll never have enough clothes to avoid this kind of problem. I simply won't. Even now that we can afford it."

Evening gowns, fancy ones such as Mother had to wear, could cost hundreds of dollars—more than tuition at my school. More than one of our housemaids earned in a year. Even Sister, with all the money her grandparents sent her, didn't have many gowns, and most of hers she had worn as a bridesmaid for one of our cousins' weddings.

"You'd rather spend the money on something else," I said.

"I would," Mother replied. "I'd rather buy a horse. Or take a trip somewhere. Really, my wardrobe is perfectly adequate."

"Well," said Miss Hagner, twisting a stray wisp of hair and tucking it behind her ear, "let's see. Last time I wrote that you would be wearing pale blue silk with a gored skirt and scoop neckline accented with ribbon and a row of Vichy lace. What's another word for that blue? Sky blue?"

"No," Mother said. " 'Sky blue' does not sound dignified."

"Palest cornflower," I said. I loved Mother's blue dress.

"Cornflower! Very good!" said Miss Hagner. She wrote it
down.

"And don't mention the lace," Mother said. "Say something about the train instead, or the trim on the skirt."

Miss Hagner scribbled. "Here we go. 'Tonight Mrs. Roosevelt will wear a formal gown of palest cornflower, with a
medium-length train trimmed in rosettes of light blue ribbon. The bodice features matching rosettes. To offset the
whole she will carry white starburst chrysanthemums.'
There. That should hold them." Mother nodded. Miss
Hagner turned to her typewriter and made an official copy.

Mother stood. "Come, dear. Let's see if Kermit's home
and your father is ready for our ride."

As we went down the hall I asked her, "Do you mind being the wife of the president?"

"Mind? No, of course not. It's exciting. We get to give
lovely dinners, and now we can afford to buy all the books
we want." She tweaked my hair. "What do you think? How
do you like it so far?"

I skipped a few steps. "I like it *here* all right," I began.

"Don't talk to me about your school yet," Mother said.
"You need to give it time."

I stopped and looked at her. "I suppose I'm not used to
any of it yet," I said. "I didn't expect Father to be president."

Mother smiled. "Do you know what?" she said. "I did.

Not the way it happened, of course. But I always thought he was destined for something like this. Even when I was a girl I thought he was different from every other boy I knew." She took my hand. "Come. Kermit must be home by now. We need to wish him happy birthday."

Thursday had been Kermit's twelfth birthday. We sang to him before dinner Friday night, but we saved our main celebration for a gala lunch on Saturday. Our cook made a tall cake frosted with white sugar icing, and I decorated it all over with tiny yellow chrysanthemums from the garden. Two of Kermit's new schoolmates came to lunch.

Kermit already had two friends. They were nice boys, too. They had good table manners, they spoke politely to Mother and Father, and they wrestled with Archie and Quentin in the hall. One was named Alan and one was named Rob. I envied Kermit.

"Well!" Father said, wiping his mustache with his napkin when we were done with the cake. "What have you fellows got planned for the afternoon?"

"We don't know yet, sir," replied Alan.

"What would you say to a nice walk around Rock Creek Park with me, then? A sort of a scramble?"

"Oh, yes, sir!" said Alan.

"Thank you, sir!" said Rob.

"He doesn't mean a *walk*," I said. "A scramble means going through creeks and up cliffs and things. You might not like it. You'll ruin your clothes." Our scrambles were always on foot, through the wildest terrain Father could find. Alan and Rob were all dressed up.

"We don't mind, sir," said Alan, still talking to Father. Looking at his and Rob's faces, I realized that they weren't really talking to my father at all. They were talking to *Theodore Roosevelt, president of the United States*. I looked at Kermit to see if he cared. He was smiling, and his eyes sparkled. I would probably be happy too, if I had two friends already. "We love to go on walks. Or scrambles," Alan added, grinning at me. "We don't mind a little dirt."

I hated to be grinned at. I picked at the pattern on the plates with my fork.

"Bully!" Father said. He stood up from the table. The boys stood too.

"I'll loan them some of my old clothes," Kermit suggested. "Come on!" He dashed away, with Alan and Rob close behind.

I sat. "Ethel?" Kermit's voice floated down the stairs. "Aren't you coming? Hurry up!"

I got up and ran after them, almost dizzy from the relief of not being left behind. I always went on scrambles at home, but I'd been afraid Kermit wouldn't want me now that he had friends.

Behind me Archie began to wail. "I want to come! Let me come too!"

"Oh, all right," Father said. "You're a fine sturdy boy. I suppose you can keep up."

"Hooray!" Archie leapt up, and Quentin began to wail.

"*No,*" Mother told him.

"Come, Quentin," Miss Young said. "We'll go out and see the guinea pigs, and then we'll have a story."

* * *

In my bedroom I changed quickly. Mother didn't fuss much over clothes, but I knew better than to go on one of Father's scrambles in anything but an old dress and strong wool stockings.

On our way out we ran into two men in suits, and our uncle Will. They were all coming to see Father. "Children, meet the junior senator from Illinois and the ambassador from France," Father said. He told us their names, but I forgot them immediately. It didn't matter; I could call them Mr. Senator and Mr. Ambassador and no one would mind. Mother taught me that; she said it made things easier. "We're just going for a little walk," Father told them. "Come along!" Uncle Will shook his head, laughing, but the others looked pleased and came with us.

We took the big carriage to Rock Creek Park. Father started the scramble gently, through a field and then a stretch of woods with hardly any brambles, though he was walking as fast as he could. The boys and I trotted to keep up. The French ambassador looked pained.

Archie jogged beside me. "Over, under, or through," he panted, "but never around." That was Father's motto; we'd learned it well on our scrambles near Sagamore, where Father liked to take us over Cooper's Bluff, especially when the tide was high.

"Here we go," Father said cheerily, and I knew the real fun was starting. Father cut straight into the deep woods and headed down a rock-strewn ravine. Not for nothing was it named Rock Creek Park. We clambered over rocks taller than me. We wriggled between boulders. Archie tumbled headlong into the underbrush and came up covered in brambles. The French ambassador lost a shoe. I helped him find it. "*Merci,*" he said politely. "Your walks, are they always so strenuous?"

"Oh, no," I said. "They get much harder."

We reached the bottom of the ravine, where the water was. This was one of the reasons I'd worn wool stockings; it was cold for mid-October, and Father was bound to get us wet somewhere. We splashed through the creek. The senator tried to creep across on top of the rocks. He fell in. The water wasn't deep, but it was deep enough to make him mostly wet. Father helped him out. "Too much for you?" he asked. "Shall we go back?"

The senator looked at Father. Then he looked at me. I was still mostly dry, except for my shoes, and I hadn't fallen once. The senator grinned ruefully. "Of course not," he said. "Aren't we having fun!"

I was having terrific fun. We came to a downed tree I couldn't quite climb over. I got down on my belly and scooted under it. Father and Kermit cheered. Archie followed me. The only clean part of him was his eyes.

It was twilight by the time we headed home. The French ambassador's suit was mud stained and torn; the senator's clothes were still wet, and he looked as if he was clenching his teeth to keep them from chattering. Father was warm and happy. He held me on his lap in the carriage. I put my head against his chest. He smelled like wet wool and shaving soap. "Did you have fun, dearest Ethel?" he asked.

"Yes," I said. "Yes."

* * *

"Please don't make me go back to school," I begged at breakfast on Monday. "I'll learn better at home. I'll learn faster. I promise."

Father chuckled. "It's a fine school, Ethie. You'll get used to it."

"Give it time, dear," Mother said serenely.

"Do I have to?"

Father and Mother exchanged calm glances. "Yes," Mother said. "You do."

Quentin was sitting straight across from me, scooping up big globs of jelly with a spoon. He looked wide-eyed. "Won't you miss me, Quenty?" I said.

He took the spoon from his mouth. "Not especially," he said.

17

At school we did not get newspapers, but of course the day girls could read them at home. By Friday noon the whole school was buzzing about something. Girls whispered among themselves as we lined up for the lunch procession; they looked at me, then looked away. I was used to being stared at by some of them. I was not used to being noticed by everyone. When we filed past the principals' dais, Miss Bangs pressed her lips together and looked at me with sympathy. It made me nervous. Miss Bangs wasn't usually sympathetic.

"Do you know what your father *did?*" Harriet asked me when we were seated and grace had been said.

"No, what?" I looked quickly toward the principals. Surely if there had been trouble Miss Bangs would have told me. "Did something happen? Was he hurt?"

Harriet sneered. "Of course he wasn't hurt. Who would hurt him?"

The same sort of person who would hurt President McKinley. I didn't say anything. My heart thumped.

"On Wednesday night," said Gertrude, also sneering, "your father ate dinner with a—"

"That's enough," Miss Mallett said firmly. "I think today we should practice our German. Emily, lead us off. Ask Harriet a question." Emily sighed and stumbled through a line of German from one of our first exercises. She asked Harriet her name. Harriet replied with a long, beautifully pronounced sentence that didn't seem to contain her name at all, or any other words I recognized. I wondered how to say *insufferable show-off* in German, and who Father had eaten dinner with, and why anyone should care.

* * *

After lunch I thought of asking someone about Father, but I didn't. When I went up the stairs to get my books for my afternoon classes, a knot of girls at the top shushed themselves and started giggling the moment they saw me. I wouldn't give them the satisfaction of speaking to them after that. If something was wrong with Father, I would find out when I got home.

School was almost out. I waited in a fever of impatience. When our last class was over I raced for the stairs. Emily was right in front of me, climbing slowly. I danced up and down on the step, wanting to push past her but not wanting to be rude. I knew Emily thought I was rude already, from the way I'd spoken to her Monday. Somehow during the whole week that had gone by, I hadn't made amends.

"Hey," I said to her. "Aren't you glad it's Friday?"

She turned and paused. "Are you leaving again?" she asked.

"Yes," I said. "When are you allowed to go home?" Almost all the other boarders stayed for the weekends, but they had to go home sometime.

She made a face. "Christmas."

"Not Thanksgiving?"

Emily got a look on her face as if she was trying not to cry. "At Thanksgiving we have only one day off. I live too far away. I can't get home and back again that fast." She sniffed. "Mother said she'd make it up to me at Christmas."

"That's horrible," I said.

Emily nodded. "But Mother writes me nearly every day."

Mother wrote me nearly every day too. Father wrote me two or three letters a week, funny ones with little drawings of our animals. Ted and Kermit wrote sometimes, Sister almost every week.

I could tell Emily liked school better than I did. She did well in almost all her classes. She was much better at the piano than I was—she practiced every evening for an hour, while I mostly used my free time for reading. But she also seemed as homesick as I was, and she wouldn't see her family for two and a half months.

"I love letters," I said, "but they're not the same."

Emily's eyes filled with tears. "I have to go," she said. She wiped her sleeve across her eyes and ran the last few steps to her bedroom door. I went out to the carriage that was waiting for me, feeling so awful for Emily that I completely forgot the girls had been whispering about Father.

The next morning there weren't any newspapers on the breakfast table, and when Father rang for them, Mr. Hoover himself answered the bell.

"Not this morning, Mr. President," he said politely but firmly. "Not with the children at the table."

Kermit and I exchanged puzzled glances. Archie, lining up a row of sugar cubes in battle formation, didn't look up. Mother sighed. "Very well. Have them sent up to my library. Theodore and I will read them later."

Father stabbed his bacon.

"Is it because of Mr. Washington?" Kermit asked.

"Washington?" I said. "What's he got to do with it?"

"Not President Washington," Kermit said. "Booker T. Washington. He ate dinner here on Wednesday night."

"Oh," I said. "Is that what everybody at school was whispering about?"

Mother shook her head sadly. "I suppose so," she said.

"Is he some kind of criminal?"

"No, Ethel," Kermit said. "He's a Negro."

I knew *Negro* was the polite word for a person with black skin. "Is that all?" I asked.

"Mr. Booker T. Washington," Father said sternly, "is an educated, genteel, and extremely intelligent man. He did this house honor. He came for a private meal and I greatly enjoyed our conversation." Father adjusted his spectacles. "That is all I have to say."

I didn't expect him to say more. Father almost never spoke to us about his dinner guests. But I didn't expect him to look so agitated, either. Kermit sighed. When Father wasn't looking, Kermit shook his head.

* * *

I sneaked up to Mother's library later and read what Mr. Hoover thought I shouldn't. The papers said the most awful things. I had seen all sorts of men and women visit the White House. Anyone who was properly dressed could ask permission to speak to Father. But dining with him, it seemed, was another matter. The idea of Mr. Booker T. Washington's eating dinner with Father made people angry. He could do what he liked in his own home, one paper said, but not in the home of the president of the United States.

One paper wondered if Mother's knees had touched Mr. Washington's under the table while they ate. One said Father was an affront to all southern women, including his own mother, who had been born in Georgia.

Mother came in as I was reading. I was so shocked by the hateful words in the papers that I forgot I wasn't supposed to be reading them. I looked at Mother. "I don't understand," I said. "Father and Kermit say Mr. Washington is a great man."

Mother put her arms around me. "He is," she said. "But in this supposedly civilized society, prejudice runs wide and deep."

"But isn't Father the president of everyone?"

I meant that he was president of Booker T. Washington, too, but Mother sighed and said, "Yes. He is the president of those inflammatory bigots, whether they like it or not. Don't worry about it, Ethel. It'll pass."

"Would Grandmother really be ashamed?" I asked.

Mother took the newspaper out of my hand. She stacked the papers together and slid them out of sight between her desk and the wall. "Your grandmother Roosevelt?" she asked.

I nodded.

"She was from the South," Mother said. "I honestly don't know what her views on this matter would have been. But she was more gracious and had better true manners than any woman I've known. When I was a young girl my family didn't have the money to hire a tutor, so your grandmother arranged for me to study alongside your aunt Corinne. Your grandmother never made me feel as if I were taking charity. I always felt welcome in her home. If she had been at dinner with us and Mr. Washington, she would have made him feel welcome, I'm sure."

* * *

Yet Father still seemed troubled. "He didn't do anything wrong," Kermit said. We were up on the roof of the White

House. Kermit had discovered a stairwell near Miss Young's new bedroom that led there from the attic. The roof of the White House was flat, with a high wall around it, and when I stood on my toes to peek over the edge, I could see for miles all around—buildings and people and the green strip of grass called the Mall. No one knew we were up there. It was the perfect place for private conversations.

"He didn't, and he knows it," continued Kermit. "But he hates for people to think he did the wrong thing."

"If he knows he's right, he shouldn't worry about what people think. Or say," I added.

Kermit snorted. "You know that isn't true. Anyway, it does matter what people think about Father. If people don't respect him because of this, they won't listen to him about important things. Like the canal he wants dug in Panama. Like the trusts and monopolies. Congress has to be happy with him. Everyone does."

"That's stupid," I said to Kermit.

He nodded. "But it's true."

I still didn't understand why talking to Father in his office was acceptable but eating dinner with him was not. Kermit explained, "Eating dinner with Mr. Washington—sitting down at a table with him—means Father was treating him as an equal."

On one hand, I didn't think anyone was equal to Father. On the other hand, Father and Mother dined with people almost every night. I remembered Mother complaining about some of the councilmen in Albany who smelled bad and had terrible manners. If they were Father's equals, then

Mr. Washington should be too. "Well, of course," Kermit replied when I said as much. "But some people don't see it that way."

* * *

The Sunday papers were worse. Editorials pointed out once again that Father's mother had been a southern woman and that Father was insulting her, Mother, and every white woman in America. Mother did not look as if she felt insulted. But for the first time since we'd come to the White House, Father wasn't smiling.

"Can't talk about that, miss," Arthur said when I asked him about it on the drive back to school Monday morning. "I got no opinions. Don't ask me no more."

Father had left the breakfast table early. He was taking a train to Connecticut to speak at Yale University. Father had gone to Harvard, and all my brothers were going to go to Harvard too. "Do you mind going to Yale?" I teased him.

He furrowed his brow. "No, no, of course not," he said, missing my joke entirely. He mopped his mustache with his napkin, kissed us all distractedly, and rushed off with Mr. Craig and Mr. Loeb at his heels.

"Never mind," Mother said. "It'll all blow over soon."

At school it had not blown over a whit. When I rushed upstairs with my things, Emily grabbed my arm and whispered, "All weekend they were saying such terrible things!"

I yanked my arm away and glared at her. She looked hurt. "I just thought you should know," she said.

"Why would I want to know something like that?" I said. I narrowed my eyes at her. "I'm surprised at you, repeating tales." Oh, how I wanted to be home! I threw my things into my room and rushed downstairs. When I ran into the classroom the other students went absolutely still. No one said a word. No one even looked at me.

At lunch no one talked. Emily stared at her plate. The other girls exchanged glances. Even Miss Mallett couldn't keep the conversation going. "I suppose silence is golden," she said at last, giving up.

I didn't understand until we'd been given permission to leave our places. Under the noise of the scraping chairs, Harriet muttered, "Miss Bangs said we weren't to speak to you about your father's actions. Well, then we aren't going to speak to you at all!"

I felt my eyes fill with tears. I fought crying. I wouldn't, in front of Harriet. She began to smile, a slow, smug smile, and I felt a surge of anger well up in place of my tears. I smiled back, a fierce, glittering smile.

Then I kicked her in the shins as hard as I could.

* * *

After I had sat for an hour on the wooden bench in the hallway outside her office, Miss Bangs let me come inside.

"Ethel," she said not unkindly, "we do not resort to physical violence in this school."

I didn't say anything, though I didn't think it was fair. I never got in trouble when I kicked Kermit.

Then I felt a ray of golden hope shooting from my heart. "Am I going to be expelled?" I asked. *Oh, please.*

Miss Bangs shook her head. "No," she said. "Though we

would of course expel any student we found to be permanently out of harmony with her surroundings."

"I'm out of harmony," I said.

"You're adjusting," she said. "You're doing fine, Ethel. But you may not kick Harriet."

"But she said—"

Miss Bangs held up her hand. "I don't care. You may not kick her, or hit her, or anyone else in this school, for that matter. The next time you do, I will not allow you to go home for the weekend. Do you understand?"

"Yes, ma'am. But she said—"

"Ethel. That's all."

I got up, smoldering with anger.

* * *

At dinner Emily took a deep breath and began, "Ethel, did you like—"

Harriet shot a look at Gertrude, who elbowed Emily. "Hey—" said Emily.

"Girls!" said Miss Mallett.

I put down my fork, looked at Harriet, the cause of the trouble, and said, "My father is the president of the United States. He may invite whomever he chooses to dine, and that person cannot in politeness refuse. Anyway, it wasn't a state dinner, it was a private meal."

"Well," snapped Harriet, "all I know is that my father would never invite someone like that to *our* house, let alone for dinner."

Neither one of us said Mr. Washington's name. But

everyone at our table—and at the tables surrounding ours, to judge by the sudden silence in the room—knew who we were talking about.

"No," I agreed, "I don't suppose many intelligent, well-educated gentlemen come to your house."

Harriet gasped. So did half the room. Miss Mallett said, "Ethel! For shame!" I smiled at Harriet and went back to my meal. As I reached for my glass of milk, I looked up at the principals' dais. Miss Bangs caught my eye. Her lips weren't smiling, but her eyes were.

I didn't get into trouble at all.

* * *

The only problem was that too many of the girls had heard me say "My father is the president of the United States." I hadn't been bragging. I'd been defending Father. Yet now they said I was proud and boastful.

"She must think she's something special," a quiet girl named Sophie whispered to Emily as we got up. Emily didn't look at me, but she nodded. My heart sank.

* * *

"Why don't you invite all of us to the White House, then?" Gertrude asked me the next morning. "After all, we wouldn't dare refuse."

"I can't," I said.

"Won't your father, the president, let you?"

"No," I said. *You aren't my friends.*

I was never so glad to leave school as I was that Friday. I burst out the door and ran down the steps. Arthur lifted me onto the box, laughing. "Miss Ethel!" he said. "Don't you look like a spring morning!"

"I can't look like spring," I said. It was late October; the leaves were turning brown and gold.

"You do. All that happiness."

"It's because I'm going home."

Arthur smiled and put the reins into my hands. I slapped the horses into a trot, and he didn't make me pull them back. "Got another surprise for you at home," he said.

"More horses?"

"No, miss."

I turned to look at him. "What? A new dog?"

"No, miss. Watch the road, now, if you're going to drive."

"Another guinea pig had babies."

"No."

"Quentin broke his arm."

"No, miss. It's a good surprise. Least I figure you'll think so."

"The emperor of Abyssinia really is going to send us a zebra and a lion!"

Arthur chuckled. "I believe he is—but Mrs. Roosevelt says they have to go to the zoo."

"Rats." We'd been offered all sorts of gifts in honor of Father's presidency, but the zebra was the best. I thought a zebra could be very happy grazing on the White House lawn.

"What is it, Arthur? Tell me."

"No, I think I'll let you see for yourself."

I begged and pleaded the whole drive home, but Arthur wouldn't give in. He pulled up to the front door of the White House. "Hop down, now, and run and see your mother. I believe that's where you'll find your surprise."

I took the front steps two at a time, dodged some important-looking gentlemen in the Cross Hall, waved at Tom Pen, nearly ran smack into Secretary Hay, who was always visiting Father, and thundered up the stairs to the family quarters. I threw open Mother's library door. "I'm home! Arthur said there was— *Sister!*"

She was sitting on the floor in front of Mother's desk. She stood up when she saw me, and I launched myself at her. "Ethel! Whoa, careful, honey!" Sister staggered to the divan and pulled me onto her lap. I was too big for that, of course, but I laughed and hugged her all the same. "How sweet you look!" she said. "I've missed you!"

"I've missed you, too!" I told her. "I've missed you for ages. I wish you'd come to school with me."

"Hello, Ethel," Mother said quietly. She had a funny look on her face, one she got only when Sister was around.

"Hello, Mother," I said.

Sister wore a white skirt and a white blouse, and her hat had beautiful white silk flowers on the brim. She looked so trim and pretty. Her wide-set eyes, which I had always admired, glittered with amusement. "Is school any better?" she asked. "Any less dreadful?"

I shook my head.

"Then I'd better not try it. If you don't like it, I'm sure I wouldn't be able to bear it. Anyway, I don't want to. Look, I brought you something from New Haven." She plucked a parcel off the floor and gave it to me. Inside was a purple felt banner reading YALE. "It's from the university," she explained. "I went with Father to the dinner where he spoke."

"Thank you!" I stroked the banner, then folded it carefully. "I'll take it to school and hang it in my room." It would look just right there. Sister must have known it was the sort of thing all the girls had. She knew how to do everything right. "I'll show it to Emily on Monday," I said.

"Is that the girl you were rude to?" Sister asked. "The one you wrote to me about?"

I flushed. I'd been rude to Emily more than once, but never exactly on purpose. "I like her best of all the girls," I said. "I'm going to try to be nicer."

"Of course you are!" Sister said. "I'm sure she likes you, anyway. How couldn't she? My lovely darling sister!"

A warm feeling, almost a glow, spread through me. I giggled. Sister giggled back.

Mother had finished stacking the papers on her desk. She looked up. "We need to get changed now," she said. "We're meeting your father at the stables in half an hour."

"Are you coming?" I asked Sister.

"I am!"

I took Sister's arm and we skipped off to our rooms. I took her through mine first and showed her the door that connected them. "You've got the bigger one," I said, opening the door. To my surprise, I saw that her trunks were already unpacked. "When did you get here?" I asked.

"Yesterday morning. Father and I took the night train from New Haven. Didn't they tell you I was coming?"

"No," I said.

She frowned. "Mother knew last week. And Father did too, he cabled me at Aunt Bamie's to say when I should be ready."

"They just wanted to surprise me." I sat on Sister's bed and bounced up and down.

"That or they were afraid I wouldn't come."

I stopped bouncing. "Did *you* think you wouldn't come?"

Sister wrinkled her nose. "I couldn't stay away forever, could I?"

"I don't know," I said. I had worried that she could.

"Silly girl." She pulled a riding habit out of her wardrobe.

"Is that new?" I asked. "It's beautiful."

Sister stroked the smooth navy wool. "Grandpa Lee bought it for me."

"That's nice," I said.

She turned and smiled. "It's nicer still that you missed me. I know you really did. I can tell!"

* * *

With Sister there I had to ride Diamond, Father's old polo pony, who was practically a hundred years old and could barely stagger. I had wondered why we'd brought him to Washington at all. Sister got Wyoming. "Can't I ride Renown?" I asked. Kermit had him, but for once he could take old Diamond instead of me.

"Not in a sidesaddle," Father said. "Renown's not trained for it. You could ride him astride—"

Mother cut in. "No."

"You take Wyoming," Sister offered. "I'll ride Diamond."

"No, no," Father said cheerfully. "You'll have more fun on Wyoming. Ethel doesn't mind. Do you, Ethel?"

Father looked happy for the first time since Mr. Washington had come to dinner. How could I mind?

Sister, who looked happy too, rolled her eyes at me. "Don't worry," she whispered, "you know I won't ride very often." She rode because we all rode, because Father expected us to. She very nearly hated horses. "They're so twitchy and quick," she'd said once.

"Like you," I had replied, and she'd laughed. She looked graceful in the saddle, and she never refused any fence that Father would take first, but she didn't love riding, she dreaded it. Her face grew paler and her eyes wider. She bossed her horses not firmly, the way they ought to be bossed, but fearfully. Fortunately, ours were not the sort of horses to take advantage, except Algonquin, perhaps, and Sister had outgrown him long before.

"I'll stay back with Ethel," she said now as we started out.

"Ride up here with me!" Father said. He and Bleistein surged ahead. Bleistein was lovely. "Come see my new horse, Sister! Come on!"

Sister's face lit with a quick smile. She spurred Wyoming on, and I was left with Mr. Gilbert, the rear-guard policeman. He had to pull his heavy hunter up to stay with me.

Diamond leaned into my hands and ignored my leg altogether. He was old, but he wasn't as incapable as he liked to pretend. "You stubborn beast." I smacked him with my whip. He jolted forward, offended, then lapsed back into a petulant trot. "I can't stand this horse," I said to Mr. Gilbert.

He eyed Sister, cantering ahead with Father and Mother. "Kind of hard, is it?" he said. "The older kids come home and steal all your fun."

I blinked. "It's not hard," I said. I would have preferred Wyoming, true. But I wasn't jealous of Sister. It would have been hard to envy her, knowing that her mother had died, knowing that so many secrets in our family existed because of her. Besides, I was happy she'd come home. Sister was fun to be around.

On Saturday Mother began to make plans for Sister's debut. This was the big party that would launch her into proper society; she would be almost a grown-up afterward. Mother was pleased. Sister's debut would be held the night of January 2, right after the New Year's reception that would mark both the opening of the social season and the end of the official mourning for President McKinley.

"Do we have to have it here?" Sister asked. We were sitting in the East Room, where Mr. Hoover had brought us tea.

Mother looked shocked. "It's the president's house. Of course we must have it here."

"But it's hideous," Sister said.

The weather had grown colder, so we had to keep the windows shut. The White House was gloomy as an Egyptian tomb. Musty smells had returned. The elaborate rococo fixtures of the East Room glimmered in the flickering gaslight. The extra flowers Mother had ordered did little to improve the atmosphere. I could see Sister's point.

State dinners were one thing. "It's not cheerful enough for a real party," I said.

Sister shot me a grateful look. "See?" she said. "Ethel thinks so. It's not just me." She sniffed, looking around. "This room is all late Grant and early Pullman," she said.

It was true. Grant, who had been president twenty years before, could be blamed for most of the ugly furniture. Mother said styles were different then. And much of the White House did look like a Pullman railroad car, especially the State Dining Room, with all that purple velvet and the carpets worn thin.

"I agree." Mother sighed. "For one thing, the ceiling in this room has got to be replaced. We need more light, more dignity. We ought to put in electricity. We also need a dining room that can seat a large group of people, not the pokey broken-up thing we have now. And your father wants a place to hang his trophies."

Father's trophies were the stuffed heads of animals he'd killed on his hunts. He had a lot of them. "*No,*" Sister said. "We are not having that moth-eaten buffalo head staring down at people during my debut."

"I like the buffalo head," I said. "It's my favorite." Father was very proud of it. I loved hearing him tell about his buffalo hunt.

"Absolutely not," Sister said. "No dead animals."

Mother pursed her lips. "Very nice, Ethel, but the trophies aren't something Sister needs to worry about. I doubt very much we'll be able to make any major improvements before the debut. It's barely two months away."

Sister's eyes darted around the room. Mother jotted some notes on a piece of paper. I reached for another tea cake. Suddenly Sister burst out, "There's no dance floor! Not anywhere! All the big rooms have carpet."

I hadn't realized this, but it was true. The East Room and the State Dining Room were the only rooms big enough for a ball—but you couldn't dance properly on carpet. You had to have a wooden floor. Even I, who hadn't started dancing lessons yet, knew that.

"I know," Mother said ruefully. "I already asked Mr. Hoover about that. He said they have a special floor covering that they put over the carpet in the East Room for dances. It's waxed linen. A crash floor, he called it."

"Oh, *no*!" Sister cried. "How utterly obscene!"

"I agree it will be a bit peculiar," Mother said calmly, "but I don't see what we can do about it. Even in the money Congress gave McKinley there wasn't anything set aside for a dance floor—and of course, we haven't yet gotten permission to spend the money they did set aside." She smiled. "We're having some congressmen to dinner next week, dear. You might want to bring the subject up to them."

Sister's eyes glittered. "I will," she said. "I'll charm a dance floor out of them."

I grinned. I couldn't wait to see Sister turned loose on Congress.

* * *

Sunday was Father's forty-third birthday. Sister and I decorated a cake for him, with colored icing and sugar roses.

Halfway through the afternoon, when we were all sitting in the Red Room reading together, Mr. Hoover knocked on the door. "A birthday gift for you, Mr. President," he said. Birthday gifts had been coming all weekend, so I wondered why Mr. Hoover made such a point of this one. "Fresh possum," he said. "From some Negro admirers."

It was a kind gift—Father loved roast possum—but his face saddened as he took it. He was still unhappy most of the time about the business with Mr. Washington. "I will have anyone I wish to dine at any time I please," he had declared at breakfast, but then he shook his head, as if he wasn't really sure.

"Are you afraid people don't like you?" I asked him after he'd handed the possum back and Mr. Hoover had left the room.

"I know people don't like me," he replied. "Some people won't like a president no matter what he does. I'm just surprised that there's still this much fuss over something so small." He patted my shoulder. "Not to worry. It'll pass."

* * *

Sister came to Father's birthday supper smoking a cigarette. "Put that out!" Father thundered.

"Yes, Father." She calmly snuffed it on the edge of her saucer.

"Really!" he sputtered. "Your aunt Bamie can't have allowed you to smoke in her house!"

Sister said nothing, only smiled at Uncle Will, who had come to dinner and was sitting across the table.

"Certainly not," Uncle Will said gravely.

"Can I have one?" Archie asked.

"Of course not," Sister said. "You don't want to stunt your growth, do you? Besides, cigarettes make you vomit. At least, they made me."

Archie groaned. Kermit looked disgusted. Mother and Uncle Will did not look amused.

Then I noticed Emily Spinach, Sister's small green snake, draped over her shoulders like a scarf. Uncle Will saw Emily at the same time I did, and shook his finger at Sister. Sister patted Emily Spinach, who was quite tame, and winked at Uncle Will.

Mother didn't mind snakes at the table so long as it was a family meal. Kermit's rat always came to Saturday breakfast. Father didn't especially mind either, though he did say reprovingly, "I hope you weren't parading that poor creature all around the homes of the Four Hundred."

"Dear Emily," Sister murmured, patting the snake.

Mr. Hoover minded. He came in with a set of birthday telegrams for Father, and when he saw Emily he went right back out again. Kermit and I laughed. "Wait till he sees the king snake I'm going to buy," Kermit said.

Quentin asked if we were getting a queen snake too, so we could have prince and princess snakes. Archie said that no snake had better eat his guinea pigs.

"They're not just your guinea pigs," I said. "They're everyone's."

"Not Bishop Doane," Quentin said. "Bishop Doane is *mine*."

When coffee came Sister took another cigarette out of her reticule. Father exploded. "No!" he said. "Put it away!" His mustache quivered. "Sister, you may not smoke under this roof. Is that clear?"

Her eyes flashed, but she set the cigarette down. "Clear," she said.

Before bed Kermit and I climbed to our watch spot on the roof. There sat Sister, smoking. "You promised Father!" I said.

She blew the smoke out airily. "I promised not to smoke under his roof. I'm not under the roof, I'm on top of it."

I wished I knew how to rearrange rules the way Sister did. If I did, I'd never leave home again.

Now that Sister was home, going to school felt even more like going into exile. I went into her bedroom before I left. She was still sleeping; she didn't like to come to breakfast. I poked her. "Good-bye," I said. "I'm going now."

She opened one eye. "Bye, dearie. Give me a hug."

I hugged her. "I hate school," I said.

"I know."

"I wish I were you."

"Don't bother," she said. "When *you* make your debut they'll have a dance floor." As I eased her bedroom door shut she called, "Have a good day! Be nice to Emily!" and I smiled.

* * *

Emily had made friends with Sophie.

When I'd left school on Friday she'd been as alone as I was. When I went back on Monday she and Sophie were arm in arm. Bosom friends. No room for me.

"Uh—hello, Ethel," Emily said when she saw me.

"Hello, Ethel," said Sophie.

"Hello." I could barely speak. All my plans for befriending Emily came crashing down. On the carriage ride to school I had thought out exactly what I would say. I had planned to invite her to my room after evening study.

Now it was too late. Emily didn't need me.

Miss Bangs tapped my shoulder. "Run along, Ethel. Hurry and put your things away so you can get to class on time."

* * *

In my room I found a letter waiting from Ted, full of forced cheerfulness about the Groton football team. He didn't say anything about being lonely himself, and he acted as if I'd never told him I was lonely, even though I had. He did promise to take me fox hunting on Thanksgiving.

I would love to go fox hunting. But Thanksgiving was three weeks away, and reading Ted's letter made me late for my first class. Miss Whiton was not happy.

At lunch, Harriet was still out to get me. I had resolved not to say anything else that might sound snobbish or give offense. So when Harriet said, "Who does your father plan to have for dinner this week, Ethel? The lantern lighter from Pennsylvania Avenue?" I swallowed hard and didn't say a word.

The lantern lighter was an old white man, anyway. I knew because Archie and Quentin had gotten into trouble for following him and blowing out lights as he lit them.

On Tuesday, when Harriet said, "Interesting new frock,

Ethel, but shouldn't a girl in your position dress more fashionably?" I said nothing. All through lunch I said nothing, except when Miss Mallett made me.

On Thursday, when Harriet said, "Your sister was in the paper again. She drove an automobile through the middle of Washington without a proper chaperone," I smiled and said nothing.

That would be Sister, I thought. I wondered where she'd gotten the automobile.

On Friday afternoon I found out.

When I ran out the door, instead of Arthur and the White House carriage, I found Sister and another girl waiting for me behind the wheel of a noisy two-seater automobile. It was bright red. "Climb in!" Sister yelled above the roar of the engine.

I scrambled to open the back door. Sister shook her head. "Squeeze right up here with us!" she said. "You'll get a better view."

Sister stomped on some foot pedals and moved levers with her hands, and the auto roared off. I laughed. I'd never ridden in one before, never knew they were so loud and bumpy and wonderful. "Better than horses!" Sister shouted. "More sense!" She turned the corner and had to swerve to avoid a carriage.

"Engines haven't got any sense!" I shouted. The wind blew my hair back.

"My point exactly! They can't do what you don't want them to do!"

Sister's companion was dark-haired and pretty. "This is

Margot Cassini," Sister shouted. "Her father's Count Cassini, the Russian ambassador. It's her automobile."

"Alice is a better driver," Margot said. She spoke with an accent that was almost British, like some of Father and Mother's friends.

"Whoo-ee!" Sister shouted as we turned another corner. People stopped to stare at us. "Stuffy old bird," Sister said when a society matron lifted her skirts away from our dust.

Too soon we were back at the White House. "Here you are, then," Sister said. "Tell Mother not to expect me for dinner. I'm going out with Margot. And, Ethel—" She winked. "Don't tell her how you got home. I only told Father. Mother doesn't like me driving."

On my way into the house Tom Pen shook his head at me. "Glad to see you back in one piece, Miss Ethel. Some days I think we are living in dangerous times."

"Oh, no," I said. "It wasn't dangerous. It was wonderful!"

Mother's secretary, Belle Hagner, didn't usually work on weekends, but this Saturday afternoon she came to attend to Mother's correspondence. She told me she'd been sick earlier in the week. "I'm glad you're better now," I said. I was curled up on the sofa in Mother's office, reading a book.

Belle smiled. "Thank you," she said. "How was your week?"

I grimaced. "I've decided the less I talk when I'm there, and the less I think about it when I'm here, the better off I am."

"But isn't that—" Belle started.

Mother hurried into the room. "Good afternoon, Belle. We'll have to be quick, I don't have much time."

I went back to my book, half listening to them discuss parties, invitations, and the unfortunate necessity of sending unsuitable gifts away. Mother didn't mind accepting suitable gifts, like horses or pears or possums, but things like zebras went to the zoo. I still thought the zebra would have liked us.

Sister breezed in. She moved my feet off the sofa and sat down. "Good morning," she said.

"Afternoon," Mother corrected her. "Are you just now waking?"

Sister checked the watch pinned to her waist. "Oh, heavens, no, I've been up for hours." She winked at me.

"I've written some thank-you notes on your behalf, dear," Miss Hagner said. "I hope you don't mind."

I snorted. The idea that Sister might mind having her work done for her was hilarious. Sister laughed and tickled my feet. "Monkey girl!" she said.

"All right, then," Mother said, to quiet us. "Miss Hagner hates to discuss my dress situation, but we've got a press release to write for tonight's dinner. Sister, some congressmen are coming. I expect you to be there."

Sister and Ted were both old enough to go to the dinners Mother and Father held. I wished I were.

"To get them to vote for my dance floor," Sister said. "Yes, I will."

"I suppose I'd better put your dress into the press release too, then," Miss Hagner said. "What will you be wearing, dear? Your white gown with the picot edging?"

"Good gracious, no," Sister said. "You put that in the press release last week."

Mother frowned. "Of everything you have, I think it's most suitable."

"Oh, I know I'll have to wear it," Sister said. "But I'm not describing it to the press. The last thing I need is for every person in the United States to be able to count exactly how many good dresses I own." She scooted down the sofa until she was taking up more than half the space. I sat up. "Write this," Sister said, "Miss Alice Roosevelt will be wearing a gown of crimson sateen—"

"Not crimson," Mother said. "Crimson would make you look sallow."

"Leaf green, then," said Sister. "Miss Alice Roosevelt will be wearing a gown of leaf green silk brocade, with elbow-length sleeves, a high collar, and a half train. The bodice is trimmed with a single velvet ribbon in darker green, and the dress features a wide sash of the silk brocade. Her headdress, shoes, and handbag are made to match."

If I shut my eyes, I could see Sister sweeping down the long staircase in a rustling green gown, her steps careful, her head held high.

I opened my eyes. Miss Hagner was looking at Mother, her pen motionless, her eyebrows raised. Mother nodded. "Write it down," she said. "This obsession with our clothes has become such a game. It might as well be a true charade." She turned to Sister. "What shall I wear?"

Sister smiled, a rare smile for her that lit her whole face. "Mrs. Theodore Roosevelt," she said slowly, "will be attired in wine-colored velvet, with a deep gathered ruffle trimming the edge of the fully gored skirt . . ."

Sister went on and on, describing Mother's imaginary dress, her shoes, her jewelry, the flowers she would carry. Mother usually carried flowers; if she held them in both hands, it gave her an excuse not to shake hands with strangers, which she didn't like to do. The rest of the outfit was pure fiction. Mother smiled, and Miss Hagner wrote down every word.

I watched from the stairs that night as Mother and Sister swept into dinner, Mother wearing her old blue dress and Sister wearing her old white one. But the newspaper reporters weren't invited to dinner. In the descriptions they printed in the society pages, Mother presided in wine-colored velvet, while Alice, that lovely girl, wore leaf green.

I doubt Father even noticed, but if he did, he never said a word. For the longest time afterward, Sister wrote all the dress descriptions for the press, until Miss Hagner learned the trick of making up a whole outfit. According to the newspaper reports, Mother and Sister had wardrobes overflowing with the most beautiful gowns imaginable; they never wore the same dress twice. "Just you wait," Sister told me. "When you grow up, I'll imagine some wonderful dresses for you."

Sunday evening at dinner I started to cry. I couldn't help it. I was still so lonely at school. I dreaded going back.

Father chucked me under the chin. "Enough, now. You've stated your position plainly. You know you've got to go back."

"No one likes me there," I said.

"Nonsense! Of course they do!"

"I'm sure that the other girls are just as lonely as you are," Mother said. "It shouldn't be too much trouble to make friends."

Mother had never been to school. No one knew what it was like, except Ted, who was away, and Kermit, who shrugged and said he was getting used to it and he guessed I would in time.

"I don't want to," I said.

"Ethel." Father's gentle voice had an edge to it. "Surely you're not afraid?"

* * *

I went to bed early and kept my light on so that I could read. Miss Young had loaned me *A Tale of Two Cities*. My satchel and a suitcase with some warmer clothes in it were lined up next to the door. When Sister came home, she went through my room to use the bathroom and knocked my book bag out of the way.

"Stop bothering my things," I said.

"*Tch*, what's gotten into you?"

I had to go to school, and she did not. "You know what's wrong with me," I said. "You do!"

"Ethel?" She sat on the edge of my bed. I reached up and smacked her shoulder with my fist.

"Nobody's listening to me!" I said. "Nobody! I don't want to go back to school! I didn't want to go there in the first place! I want to stay home like you!"

Sister pushed me over and moved next to me. She put her arms around me. "I know," she said.

"They let you get away with things," I said.

"You wouldn't want to be me."

The gaslights hissed softly. The tap in the water basin dripped. I could hear muffled thumps coming from Archie and Quentin's room down the hall. I thought I could hear the beating of my own heart. Sister wrapped her arms around me more tightly. "You wouldn't trade places with me, not really," she said.

"I guess not. I just wish I could be like you."

She laughed softly, her breath ruffling my hair.

"You don't," she said. "But never mind. What's the number one worst thing about school? That you can fix, I mean. Not the fact that you have to go."

I thought for a moment. The worst thing was worrying about Father, but I worried about him even when I wasn't at school, and anyway, I couldn't fix that. I thought of Harriet. I thought of being away from home and missing Mother and Father and the boys. I knew I couldn't change any of that, either.

I said, "I want to make a friend. I missed my chance to be friends with Emily."

Sister frowned. "Why? You said you were going to be nice to her this week."

"I was. But it doesn't matter. She's already friends with Sophie."

"So make friends with Sophie, too!"

"That's harder—twice as hard. I just want one friend."

"Is there anyone else you'd rather be friends with?"

I shook my head.

"So make two friends. It sounds as if you're just scared," she said. "Scared they won't like you."

"I am not scared!"

"Are too!"

"Am not!"

"Whoa!" She caught me by my wrists and held me at arm's length so that I couldn't hit her. Sister was stronger than she looked. "Stop it. I'm only telling you the truth."

"You don't know what it's like!" I said. "You don't have any idea!"

"Of course I do," she said calmly. "I'm scared all the time."

"What do you do?"

"I just do the thing I'm most scared of."

I thought of Sister riding horses, and I knew it was true. "I can't," I said. "I'm not like you."

She sighed. "I can tell you a secret," she said. "I can make it so you're not afraid."

"How?"

"It's a pretty valuable secret. I'm not sure if I can tell you without some kind of payment."

"What?"

"A dare. You'll have to take a dare."

"What dare?"

"Give me some time. I'll think of something."

"Please tell me now!"

She got up. "No, it's nothing to be in a hurry about. I'll think it all out and tell you on Friday."

"Sister!"

She closed the bathroom door behind her. "On Friday," she said.

When she came out I had turned off the light. "Will you pick me up again?" I asked. "In the automobile?"

She grinned. "If Margot lets me," she said. "Now you've got something to look forward to, don't you? Good night."

"I always look forward to Fridays," I called after her. "It's Mondays I don't like."

"I wouldn't ride in an automobile," Harriet said with a sniff during dinner on Monday. "Noisy, smoky things. Anyway, you might break your neck." She had seen me drive off on Friday with Sister and Margot.

"I liked it," I said. "It was fun."

"They're not dignified, either," said Harriet.

I shrugged. Harriet might speak perfect German, but at least *I* wasn't afraid of automobiles. "I'm sure you won't have to ride in one if you don't want to," I said. I picked at my food with my fork.

"I'd do it," Emily declared. "I think it does look like fun."

I looked up and smiled at her. She smiled back. But after that, I didn't know what else to say. What would sound right? Was it better if I waited for her to talk first? I squirmed. Emily's smile faded.

I'd made a mistake again. When the bell rang, I walked back to my room alone. After study time that evening the girls visited each other. They squealed and laughed so much that it was hard for me to concentrate on my book, even though I kept my door firmly closed.

No one ever knocked.

I missed Mother dreadfully. I missed Father. I would ten times rather have woken up in my room at the White House than in my room at school. I liked the food better at home. I liked the people better. I would have traded Miss Bangs and Miss Whiton for Tom Pen and Arthur any day.

I kept quiet. Each day passed slowly, but each was easier. I ignored Harriet when she said rude things about Father. I ignored Gertrude. I talked as little as possible, in class and at meals. I smiled hesitantly at Emily, and once I even smiled at Sophie, but that was all. I did my homework. I practiced the piano. I finished *A Tale of Two Cities*. By Friday, even Harriet didn't have much to say to me. I was becoming invisible—but not for long.

All week I thought of Sister's promise. I was counting on it. She knew the trick of being happy, the secret of making everyone love her. She had promised to tell it to me. Her dare would be a tough one, I knew—hers always were. The secret would fix things for me, though. It would give me the courage Father expected me to have, the strength I knew I lacked. It would make me brave—if not as brave as Sister, brave enough for school.

* * *

"I'll tell you my secret," Sister said, her eyes gleaming. It was Saturday morning, and we were up on the roof with Kermit. "But first, here's what you need to do. Father's having a dinner tonight. Forty people at one long table in the East Room. I want you to crawl under the table, from one end to another, and drop a note onto Father's lap."

I blinked. Only Sister would come up with a dare like that.

"I'll do it," Kermit said. His eyes were laughing like Sister's. "I'll do it with you, Ethel."

"You can't," Sister said. "This is her dare. Hers alone." She grinned at me. "You don't look happy, Ethie. Don't you want to know my secret?"

"Mother'll kill me," I said.

"No, she won't."

"She will. Who's coming to the dinner, anyhow?"

Sister waved her hand. "Some congressmen, some senators, maybe a judge or two. And their wives. I'm sitting next to the speaker. I've got to talk him into that dance floor before it's too late."

I gulped. "The speaker of the House?" Father had introduced me to him one Friday afternoon. He was a very solemn man. He hadn't liked it at all when Tom Quartz attacked his ankle on the staircase.

"If you're careful, they won't even know you're down there," Sister said. "It's not as if I'm asking you to tap everyone's knees as you go."

"There won't be room," I said.

"There will be," said Sister.

Kermit jumped up. "Let's have a look."

* * *

We ran down to the East Room. The State Dining Room wasn't big enough to hold a table for forty people, but the East Room was. Workmen, led by Mr. Hoover, had removed all the circular upholstered chairs and set up the long table. Already they were busily setting out floral arrangements. The table was draped with cloths that hung to the floor.

"See?" said Sister. "Easy as pie."

I lifted the cloth. The table was wide, wider than I'd thought, and there probably would be enough room for me to crawl past the diners' knees. "I'll have to stay under there the whole dinner," I said.

"You can duck out when you've finished," Sister said. "One length, and a note on Father's lap. But I think you'd better get under there before the dinner starts. That part'll be easy—there's going to be a reception in the Cross Hall first. I'll jump out and tell you when they're almost ready to start seating people."

I'd be like a fly on the wall, able to hear everything— only I'd be under the table. I'd get to stay up with Father and Mother at night, just like Sister did. I grinned. "I'll do it," I said.

Miss Young fed Kermit, Archie, Quentin, and me dinner in the Family Dining Room as usual. Mother peeked in on us. She was beautifully dressed, all in white, with flowers in her hair. Kermit bounced in his chair. "Don't you think dinner tonight will be exciting?" he asked her. I tried to kick him under the table but missed.

"Pleasant, certainly," Mother said. "I don't know about exciting."

After dinner we went upstairs. Archie and Quentin got into their pajamas. Mother sat down with us on the hall sofa to read. She started with Tennyson's poem *Ulysses*, one of our favorites.

> *"I cannot rest from travel; I will drink*
> *Life to the lees. All times I have enjoy'd*
> *Greatly, have suffer'd greatly, both with those*
> *That loved me, and alone. . . ."*

Kermit's eyes half closed and his lips moved in silent unison with Mother's. Archie leaned across Mother, his eyes aglow, and even Quentin was still.

"*I am become a name.*" Father came out of his bedroom proclaiming the next line of the poem. He was dressed in formal clothes, with a white carnation in his buttonhole. "*For always roaming with a hungry heart / Much have I seen and known*"—his eyes met Mother's and both of them smiled—"*cities of men / And manners, climates, councils, governments, / Myself not least, but honor'd of them all. . . .*"

"*I am part of all that I have met,*" I quoted. Father beamed at me. Mother and the boys listened while Father and I took turns, there in the upper hallway of the White House, feeding lines of Tennyson to each other. I hadn't realized that I knew the poem so well, but I got to the end of the third stanza without missing a single word and fired off the last line, "*. . . to strive, to seek, to find, and not to yield!*" in a ringing voice.

Father stepped back and bowed to me. "He has the right of it, Tennyson does," he said, and tousled my hair.

Quentin tackled him after that, unable to be still a moment longer. Archie jumped on Quentin, and they had a great bear play right there on the rug, while Mother stood aside, smoothing her long skirts and shaking her head. Father had to rush off to change his crumpled shirt and get a fresh carnation, so it was Kermit who solemnly escorted Mother downstairs.

I took my shoes off and crept down to the East Room. Mr. Hoover saw me and gave me a quizzical look, but I pretended not to see him. The noise of the reception in the Cross Hall grew louder and louder. At last Sister poked her head in the door. "Here they come, honey!" she whispered. I dove beneath the table.

I sat close to one wide end. I drew my feet beneath me. The tablecloths were white, and the light from the flickering gas chandeliers shone faintly through them. The top of the table was decorated with flowers from the greenhouses; the room smelled like a garden. A jungle, I decided. I was sitting outside a tent in the middle of a jungle in deepest Africa, just like Father. He'd been to Egypt; he'd sailed down the Nile.

I heard Father's voice, loud and hearty, as he led the party into the room. That was a lion, I thought. An African lion. King of the jungle. And I was a lion too, younger but still strong, part of the mighty beast's pride. There were hunters abroad in the jungle tonight; the king was in danger, but I carried a warning. I could save him, if only I dared travel through the jungle at night, alone.

Chairs scraped back. Knees pushed the walls of the tent toward me. Elegant shoes peeked under the tent's edges. Danger surrounded me.

People talked. I imagined their voices as the chattering of birds and monkeys in the jungle high above me. I heard Sister exclaim, "Oh, Mr. Speaker, what intelligent things you say!" and I nearly laughed aloud.

The savory smell of meals cooked over the natives' campfires permeated the room. The monkeys and birds grew quieter. I heard the clinks of forks on china. My stomach rumbled.

In the distance, the lion roared. Time, I decided, to start my journey. I slowly eased myself onto my hands and knees and began to crawl.

The jungle trail wasn't really wide enough. Almost

immediately I bumped against some branches, which jerked away like live things. I slowed down and bumped something else; slowed further, bumped still more. The other animals were getting restless. If I didn't hurry, I would be discovered. The lion would be in peril. I sped up, crawling faster, until I reached a pair of delicate shoes I recognized: Sister's.

I couldn't help myself. I stopped and leaned against her knees. She kicked me. I pinched her ankle, gently. She pushed her napkin to the ground. "Oh, my," I heard her say. (Sister was a bird, not a monkey.) "How clumsy of me." Gracefully, she bent at the waist, picked up the edge of the tablecloth along with her napkin, and popped a piece of her dinner roll into my mouth.

I was so surprised I nearly fell over backward. I chewed the roll and swallowed. Sister tapped me with her foot. Time to move on.

If there were forty guests at the table, and Father and Mother were at the ends, then there were only nineteen people down each side, but it felt like hundreds. Every time I slowed down I bumped into more people, but when I sped up I fancied everyone could hear me scrambling.

Maybe not. The talk at the table went on without ceasing. The clinks of china and silver continued, and no one but Sister reached under the table.

Father's feet, so small given how large he was, just poked beneath the cloth. I listened for his voice. When I heard him start to speak, I lifted the edge of the cloth, stuck my note on top of his napkin, and let the cloth fall back down.

I'm here on a dare, it read. *Don't tell. Love, Ethel.*

I heard the paper crinkle as he unfolded it. Then Father himself lifted the tablecloth and looked me in the eye. "If you're playing hide-and-seek, I think Kermit will have given up by now," he whispered. His face was solemn, but his eyes twinkled. "You've been under there for the entire soup course."

"Yes, Father," I whispered.

"Hold on—your mother's looking this way. All right—now skedaddle!"

I skedaddled out the East Room door. I'd done it. I'd saved the lion. Sister owed me her secret now.

27

Sister slept late, and later. When I put my ear to the door between our bedrooms, I could hear her snore. I went down to lunch. Afterward, Father suggested a scramble. While I was upstairs changing my clothes, I suddenly couldn't bear waiting anymore.

I banged into Sister's room. She was sleeping with the sheets pulled over her head. Her maid tidied her room every day, but Sister always managed to untidy it by evening—the dress she'd worn to the dinner the night before was thrown half across a chair, half on the floor, and her shoes and stockings, handkerchief and headdress were strewn at the foot of the bed. Her dressing table was covered with little glass bottles of perfume. The whole room smelled like flowers.

I tiptoed toward her. She'd nailed the photograph of her mother by the headboard of her bed just where she had kept it at Sagamore. Sister's mother was lovely. I looked at the photo and ran my fingers over the top of the frame. Then I pulled the sheets back from Sister's head.

"Go away," she said.

"No," I said. "You owe me. I want to know the secret right now."

She opened her eyes and pulled herself up onto her elbows. "Morning," she said.

"It's not. It's past lunch."

Sister smiled. "You should have seen their faces when you ran out from under that table!" she said. "My! That old judge—what's his name—I thought his false teeth were going to hit the floor!"

Neither Mother nor Father had said a word to me about it, at breakfast or at lunch. I'd told the story to the boys so well that they were all keen to try it at the next big dinner. "Mother didn't scold me," I said.

"I saw her see you," Sister said. "She's just decided to pretend she didn't. It was good fun, wasn't it?"

"Yes, but—"

"And I believe I've got them all talked into buying us a dance floor. Now if we can only get it installed before my debut!"

"But—"

Sister put her finger on the tip of my nose. "You already know the secret, honey," she said. "Any girl who will crawl the length of the table at a dinner given by the president of the United States knows every secret to bravery and friendship I possess."

"I don't," I said. "You have to tell me. You promised."

"You do," she said. "You might not know you do, but that's not my fault. Now go away. I'm going to give you my

148

necklace of pearl beads, because you're such an awfully sweet naughty child, but you have to let me sleep." She lay back and closed her eyes.

"Tell me!" I pummeled her shoulder.

She opened one eye. "Trust me, you know. Isn't there somewhere you're supposed to be?"

The scramble! I'd forgotten. I rushed out of the room. "You have to tell me later!" I shouted as I ran down the hall.

* * *

Three miles into the wildest part of Rock Creek Park Father could find, I heard Archie behind me, panting, "Over and under, but never around." I stopped so suddenly that Kermit tripped over me. That was it. The secret. *Over and under, but never around.*

Sister was right. Father had taught us all. I already knew.

On Monday Arthur and I left for school a few minutes earlier than usual. "I'm always in such a rush that I get into trouble," I explained. Besides, I had something I needed to do.

Arthur let me drive the whole way there, even along the tricky turn to the bridge, despite the traffic that clogged the streets in the morning. We saw another motorcar—black, not bright red like Margot Cassini's—sputtering in the distance. "Would you like to drive a car someday?" I asked him.

"Sure would," he said. "Wouldn't you?"

"Yes," I said, "but I think I like horses better."

"Me too," he said. "Nothin' beats a good horse." He smiled at me. "You're looking perky today, Miss Ethel. First time you've looked perky on a Monday morning."

"I still hate school," I said. The difference was, I had my feet back under me. I knew better than to be quiet. I had remembered who I really was. Not just the president's daughter. I was Ethel Roosevelt, daughter of Edith and

Theodore, sister of Alice, Ted, Kermit, Archie, and Quentin. I was independent and strong. I was me.

* * *

After I dropped my things off in my room, I walked down the hall and knocked on Emily's door. I knew exactly which one it was. "Come in," she said.

I walked in. Emily and Sophie were sitting on Emily's rug, giggling over a piece of paper they held. They stared at me. "Oh," said Emily, sounding surprised. "Hello."

"Hello," echoed Sophie.

"Hello," I said. I sat down on the rug as if I walked into Emily's room every morning. "Did you have a good weekend? What's that?"

Sophie handed me the paper. It was a drawing of a circle of girls on chairs holding things in their laps. The middle girl was on her feet shrieking, with her hand in the air and several large drops of ink falling from her fingers. The drawing was captioned *An account of the disaster Saturday morning.*

"Did you draw it?" I asked Emily.

"Sophie did," Emily said. She held up her hand, which had one bandaged finger. "They make us learn mending and plain sewing on Saturday mornings, you know."

I nodded. I was not sorry I missed that.

"I think I'm just not cut out for sewing."

"Me either," I said. "It's the only reason I go home on weekends."

Emily looked solemn for a moment, then snorted with laughter when she realized I was joking.

"Well, I'm planning to make my living as a seamstress," Sophie said. She gave a whoop and Emily laughed harder. I grinned.

"You have to see her seams," Emily said. "They're the worst things imaginable. Miss Bangs has *fits*."

"I'll show you," Sophie promised me. "I'll show you tonight."

* * *

At noon Harriet asked me whether Father had had any un-usual guests to dinner over the weekend. Everyone else had let the matter of Booker T. Washington die down, but not Harriet. I looked her in the eye. "Harriet," I said, "don't you think asking that kind of question is terribly ill-mannered?"

Truthfully, I didn't know if it was ill-mannered or not. Perhaps polite young ladies always inquired about the president's dinner guests. But Harriet flushed and looked uncertain. *Over and under,* I thought. *Never around.*

"Did you go riding this weekend?" Emily asked me.

"Some. Yesterday we had a big walk in Rock Creek Park."

"I'm sure you enjoyed that," Miss Mallett said.

"I did," I said. "My brother Archie fell into the creek and we had to pull him out. He got awfully cold. One of Father's policemen gave him his jacket, though."

The girls at the table looked interested enough but didn't say anything. I'd hoped they would respond.

After a moment's pause, Gertrude leaned across the table to a girl named Carrie, who was a few years older than I. "Have you heard anything else about Charlie?" she asked.

Carrie's smile trembled. Tears filled her eyes. "Mother sent a telegram this morning," she said. "The doctor says he got the bone set properly. She said Charlie is going to be fine."

Around the table, everyone grinned. Emily squeezed Carrie's hand. Even Harriet looked relieved.

But I didn't know who Charlie was or what had happened to him. Emily must have seen my confusion, because she leaned forward and said, "Charlie's her little brother. He was in an accident."

"Father's carriage overturned," Carrie said. "Charlie broke his leg. He's only three."

"Oh, how awful," I said. I could imagine how miserable Quentin would be, stuck in bed with a broken leg.

"We've been praying for him all weekend," Miss Mallett said.

"If I had known," I said, "I would have prayed for him too."

Then it struck me: I should have known. If I hadn't known Charlie was hurt, at least I should have known who Charlie was. Even if I wasn't here on weekends like most of the girls, I ate meals here five days a week. I'd sat across the table from Carrie for six weeks without knowing she had a brother. I belonged to this school whether I liked it or not, but up until now I had let myself stay apart.

I'd never lived anyplace where the six most important things weren't Sister, Ted, Kermit, Ethel, Archie, and Quentin. I'd never thought about what was important to the other girls.

Dessert came—pudding—and everyone fell to eating it. I looked around the room. Six weeks, I thought, and I still wasn't sure of everyone's name. I knew the girls my age, but I didn't know them well. I had some catching up to do.

* * *

That night I finished my schoolwork at my desk. My room wasn't as plain as it had been. I had a rug and a bright coverlet, my Yale banner, and some drawings Miss Young had given me. *I need a photograph*, I thought. *One of all of us.*

Someone knocked on the door. I jumped. Whoever it was knocked again. "May I come in?"

"Sure!" I yelled.

It was Emily. "My mother sent cookies. Want one?"

"Thanks," I said. I shut the book on my desk and helped myself to a cookie from the tin she held out to me.

"Want to sit down?" I asked.

"Sure." She perched on the edge of the bed. "Want another cookie?"

"Thanks." I nibbled this one more slowly. We sat looking at each other. Emily smiled. I did too, and then plunged ahead.

"I've been thinking," I said. "I'll bet you'll be awful lonely on Thanksgiving. Would you like to come home with me?"

Emily's eyes lit up, but she shook her head. "Thanks, but I'm going home with Sophie. She asked me already."

"Oh." I looked down at my hands. "I'm sorry. I mean, I bet you'll have fun with Sophie, but—"

"I'd love to come some other time."

I looked up. "Would you really?"

"Of course," said Emily.

Happiness bubbled up from my stomach and came out as a laugh. "Good! How about—how about this weekend?"

"I'd love to," Emily said. "Only Miss Bangs will have to write my mother first to get permission. That's what she had to do for Thanksgiving."

"I'll have to ask my mother too," I said. "But maybe we could telephone. That would be faster."

"We have a telephone at home," Emily said.

"We can tell Miss Bangs it's an emergency," I said.

"Yes," said Emily, "because another sewing lesson will kill me."

"You'll die if you don't get away from school."

"Absolutely," said Emily. We laughed.

"You laugh like my mother," I said.

"Is that good?"

"Of course," I said. "How can a laugh be bad?"

"Can I meet your horses?" Emily asked. "I love to ride. Can I meet your brothers and sister?"

"You can ride Algonquin," I said. "I'll introduce you to the guinea pigs. Bring your skates, we can roller-skate in the basement. I'll show you how we go out on the roof." I took a deep breath. "On Sunday sometimes Father takes us on a walk." I wondered if Emily was up to a full scramble. Father would be gentle with her if I asked him to.

Emily's eyes widened. She clapped her hand over her mouth. "Your father!" she said. "I forgot! He's the *president*."

155

"He's mostly just my father," I said. "You'll like him."

Emily wrinkled her nose. "I'll have to dress up."

I thought of the scramble, the creeks, the mud. "Dress up for my mother," I said. "For my father you'll need old clothes. Trust me."

Emily giggled. "All right," she said. "I do."

I slipped my arm through Emily's as we ran down the stairs. I'd done it, I thought. I'd made a friend. *Over, under, or through, but never around.*

I was so pleased. Father would be too.

Ethel Roosevelt around 1902.

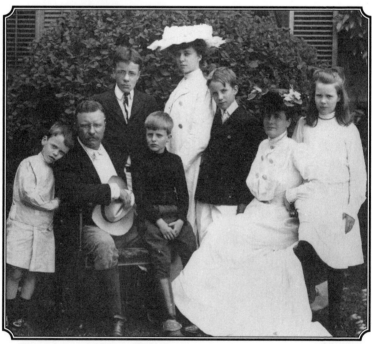

The Roosevelts at Sagamore Hill around 1903 (from left to right: Quentin, Theodore, Ted, Archie, Alice, Kermit, Edith, and Ethel).

AUTHOR'S NOTE

This book is a work of fiction, but Ethel Roosevelt really was ten years old when McKinley's death made her father, Theodore Roosevelt, the president. Her life, and the lives of all of her family, changed dramatically in an instant.

In my earliest research into the Roosevelt family, the glimpses I saw of Ethel as a child intrigued me; I felt sure I would have liked her very much. So in this book I've imagined what Ethel Roosevelt's life might have been like in the first few months after her father became president.

Ethel is less well known than other members of her family. Though many of her private letters have been preserved, no book focuses solely on her life. Her father wrote thirty-five books, including an autobiography and many volumes of personal essays, and several excellent biographies have been written about him. Edith, Alice, Ted, and other more distant family members also either published memoirs or were the subject of biographies, or both.

Nevertheless, I have made this book as true and accurate as I could. The Roosevelts were indeed staying at the remote

Tahawus Club when they received the news that President McKinley had died; the descriptions of their various journeys to Washington, of President McKinley's funeral, and of the White House as they first entered it are based on first-person accounts. The uproars over Theodore Roosevelt's dinner with Booker T. Washington, Sister's friendship with Margot Cassini, the scrambles in Rock Creek Park, Sister's creating imaginary dresses for the press, the games of "bear" before state dinners, and many other details are part of the historical record.

While facts stay the same, our opinions of them can change over time. Thus, Roosevelt forbade his daughter to smoke because it was considered rude and unladylike—not, as he might today, because of the health hazards associated with smoking. Also, it seems odd today that there was once such controversy over Roosevelt's dinner with Booker T. Washington. Before the civil rights movement of the 1960s, racial prejudice and segregation were entrenched and widespread across America. Roosevelt's attitude toward race was very enlightened for his time, but his overall views were not as progressive as most people's are today. Never again in his seven-year presidency did he invite Booker T. Washington—or any other African American—to dinner.

By any account, Theodore Roosevelt's achievements were remarkable. In 1906 he became the first U.S. citizen to win a Nobel Peace Prize, for his efforts to resolve the Russo-Japanese War. He is the only president to have been awarded the Congressional Medal of Honor, for his heroism in the Spanish-American War. An ardent conservationist, he created five national parks and eighteen national monuments (including the Grand Canyon) and put more than 230 million acres of land under federal protection. He filed more than fifteen antitrust suits to break up trade monopolies. He authorized the building of the Panama Canal. He was the first president to ride in an automobile, a submarine, and an airplane.

* * *

The National Cathedral School, which Ethel attended for five years beginning in October 1901, generously shared with me primary source material from that time. However, I don't know what Ethel's first weeks at the school were like. She was a boarder during the week and went home on weekends; her father's published letters contain repeated references to her unhappiness every Monday morning when she had to go back. On the other hand, published accounts of the school's early days describe Ethel as a happy, bubbly child. I felt that Ethel probably did learn to enjoy her life at school—she seems to have been happy by nature—but that given the choice, she would have been taught at home. She loved being with her family, and as she grew older she loved to help take care of them.

I've described the National Cathedral School itself as accurately as I could. I've kept the real names of the principals, Miss Bangs and Miss Whiton, but all of Ethel's classmates, including Emily and Harriet, are wholly fictional. Because the school still protects the records of its students,

I don't know exactly what Ethel studied or how well she did. The classes mentioned in this book are taken from the school's standard curriculum; Ethel's singing and piano lessons are mentioned in her father's letters.

Mame, Miss Young, Mr. Hoover, Tom Pen, Mr. Hay, Mr. Loeb, Mr. Craig, Belle Hagner, Pinckney, and many of the other staff members mentioned in this book are real, though I have imagined parts of their characters and all, or nearly all, of their conversations. Thomas Pendel, who retired shortly after the time I have covered in this book, wrote a book about his White House experiences in which he spoke lovingly of Tad Lincoln and the young Roosevelts. Mr. Hoover is well known for a book he wrote upon his retirement in 1933, and for his remark that "a timid person had no place" in the White House while the Roosevelts were living there.

Ethel herself recalled how, on a dare from Alice, she crawled under the table at a White House dinner. Alice really did charm congressmen into giving the money to add a dance floor to the White House; it was installed in the East Room, but, tragically, from her point of view, not until after her debut.

Some famous pranks, such as Quentin's sneaking Algonquin up the White House elevator into Archie's bedroom, and pets, such as Archie's badger, Josiah, took place or lived outside the time frame of this book. Ethel did eventually get a horse of her own, which she named Fidelity.

The young Roosevelts enjoyed the White House, but they and their mother always feared for the president's safety—much more than did the president himself. The White House police really did instruct the children to be on guard and to put themselves between their father and any perceived threat.

Theodore Roosevelt loved his children very much; he also expected a great deal from them, and they all worked hard to live up to his example. Ted, Kermit, and Archie served in World War I with distinction; Quentin died there, when the plane he was piloting was shot down over France. The remaining boys also served in World War II— Ted was the oldest soldier to land on the beaches of Normandy at D-Day. Both Ted and Kermit died during the war, though not in battle.

Of Roosevelt's daughters, Alice (always called Sister by her family) garnered the lion's share of national attention. Over and over throughout his presidency she was featured in newspapers and magazines; she was called Princess Alice, and the color of a dress she wore on one state occasion was christened Alice Blue. She served as her father's emissary on trips to Puerto Rico and the Far East, and while he was still president she married Nick Longworth, a congressman from Ohio who later became speaker of the House. Alice lived out her long life in Washington; she dined with every president through Ronald Reagan before she died in 1980.

At one time or another Alice seems to have bickered with everyone in her large family—except Ethel. In the voice-over for a video tour of Sagamore Hill that Ethel made shortly before she died, she speaks lovingly of going into Alice's bedroom, inhaling the fragrance of her perfume, and touching the glass bottles on her dressing table. They seem to have always been close.

Ethel left the National Cathedral School when she was fifteen. During the last years of her father's presidency, she helped her mother run the household and enjoyed herself much as Alice had (though less controversially). She rode, hunted, and went to parties and dances. Like her sister, she made her debut at the White House. After her father left office she spent several years helping her mother run Sagamore and accompanying her parents on trips to Europe, which she greatly enjoyed.

In 1913 Ethel married a surgeon named Richard Derby. When World War I broke out he went to France to serve in a hospital, and she went with him to serve as a nurse. She was very proud of her lifelong work with the American Red Cross.

Ethel and her husband had four children. In later years, after the deaths of her parents, she worked hard to see Sagamore Hill restored and opened to the public as a National Historic Site. Ethel Roosevelt Derby died in 1977, but thanks to her efforts, visitors from all over the world can still get a glimpse of the life and family she loved.

SELECTED SOURCES

Bishop, Joseph Bucklin, ed. *Theodore Roosevelt's Letters to His Children*. New York: Scribner's, 1919.

Derby, Ethel Roosevelt, and Sidney Kirkpatrick. *My Father the President*. A documentary video of Sagamore Hill narrated by Ethel Roosevelt Derby.

Donn, Linda. *The Roosevelt Cousins: Growing Up Together, 1882–1924*. New York: Alfred A. Knopf, 2001.

Hoover, Irwin Hood. *Forty-two Years in the White House*. Boston: Houghton Mifflin, 1934.

Lewis, Mary Key. *Polished Corners: A History of the National Cathedral School for Girls*. Mount Saint Alban, Washington, D. C., 1971.

Library of Congress. Online resources, including photographs of Ethel Roosevelt's White House bedroom and various White House rooms before the 1902 renovation. www.loc.gov.

Longworth, Alice Roosevelt. *Crowded Hours*. New York: Scribner's, 1933.

Kerr, Joan Paterson, ed. *A Bully Father: Theodore Roosevelt's Letters to His Children*. New York: Random House, 1995.

Morison, Elting, ed. *The Letters of Theodore Roosevelt*. Vol. 3. Cambridge: Harvard University Press, 1951.

Morris, Edmund. *The Rise of Theodore Roosevelt*. Rev. ed. New York: Random House, 2001.

Morris, Edmund. *Theodore Rex*. New York: Random House, 2001.

Morris, Sylvia Jukes. *Edith Kermit Roosevelt*. New York: Coward, McCann & Geoghegan, 1980.

Murphy, Eloise Cronin. *Theodore Roosevelt's Night Ride to the Presidency*. Blue Lake, New York: Adirondack Museum, 1977.

National Cathedral School for Girls, Yearbooks from 1900–1901, 1901–1902, 1902–1903.

Pendel, Thomas. *Thirty-six Years in the White House*. Washington, D.C.: Neale Publishing Company, 1902.

Roosevelt, Eleanor B. *Day Before Yesterday*. Garden City, New York: Doubleday, 1959.

Roosevelt, Theodore. *Autobiography*. New York: Scribner's, 1913.

Roosevelt, Theodore. Theodore Roosevelt's *Diaries of Boyhood and Youth*. New York: Scribner's, 1928.

Sagamore Hill National Historic Site, National Park Service.

Teague, Michael. *Mrs. L.: Conversations with Alice Roosevelt Longworth*. Garden City, New York: Doubleday, 1981.

Leonard, Barry, ed. *The White House: An Historic Guide*. Washington, D.C.: White House Historical Association, 21st edition, 2001.

ABOUT THE AUTHOR

Kimberly Brubaker Bradley has written several historical novels, and she enjoys researching the details of other times and places. Her most recent novel, *For Freedom*, was praised as "taut, engrossing" (*Booklist*, starred review) and "an exciting account of a girl's coming of age" (*School Library Journal*, starred review) and was selected for several award lists, including *Booklist*'s Top Ten Historical Fiction for Youth.

Kimberly Brubaker Bradley and her husband have two young children, Matthew and Katie. They live on a farm in eastern Tennessee, in the foothills of the Appalachian Mountains.